Mortal Clay, Stone Heart

And Other Stories in Shades of Black and White

EUGIE FOSTER

Cover Art
From "Stock 035" by ~ro-stock and ~enchanted-stock
(http://enchanted-stock.deviantart.com/gallery/3687259#/dwxzcx)

ISBN: 1-49283-699-0
ISBN-13: 978-1-49283-699-5

PRAISE FOR…

THE LIFE AND TIMES OF PENGUIN:

"Eugie Foster's 'The Life and Times of Penguin' succeeds in being, by turns, funny, thought-provoking, and poignant"
—**Douglas Hoffman**, *Tangent*

"Told from the point of view of a balloon animal penguin, the toy's brief but eventful life manages to jam in enough existential angst to give Kierkegaard indigestion, an astonishing emotional depth, and yet fully embrace the essentially absurd nature of [Eugie Foster's] story."
—**Martin McGrath**, *The Fix*

"both touching and uplifting"
—**Geoff Willmetts**, *SF Crowsnest*

"a beautiful fantasy, which employs the trappings of children's fiction, with adult emotional themes of risk and mortality."
—**Talie Helene**, *ASif*

RUNNING ON TWO LEGS:

"A wonderful story, one that I enjoyed reading tremendously. It's one of the best stories I've ever critiqued in my years of teaching writing workshops."
—**A.C. Crispin**

RUNNING ON TWO LEGS (cont.):

"a beautiful story—touching without being sentimental, with characters that come believably to life."
—Victoria Strauss

"the beauty of the language carries one along...It is difficult to write a thoughtful story that features a terminal disease without melodrama, and Eugie Foster achieves it with style."
—E. Sedia, *Tangent*

THE BUNNY OF VENGEANCE AND THE BEAR OF DEATH:

"a profoundly strange supernatural look at the morality of revenge."
—Nick Gevers, *Locus*

"the story is emotionally effective and, impressively, given its subject matter, makes its point through character and story rather than cold rhetoric."
—Ben Payne, *Tangent*

CONTENTS

THE LIFE AND TIMES OF PENGUIN

PENGUIN FELT THE breath of life enter his body. The gush of warm, slightly humid air filled him, inflating him nearly to the brim. But the Creator did not overfill him; he left some slack for his beak and tied him off in a neat knot. Penguin shivered at the pain of birth as the Creator twisted and bent him to his will, giving him shape as well as substance. But Penguin cherished it too, knowing he had been plucked from the void to be given this gift of holy suffering.

Gradually, the Creator added limbs and color to Penguin's inky-black body: bright orange feet and a shiny white breast. Penguin squealed and squeaked in anguish as he felt these parts plaited on, all the while revering the Creator in his divine wisdom. Then the Creator was done and Penguin was finished.

Penguin heard the holy words of the Creator and knew they were good.

"Here you go, sweetie, there's a nice penguin for you."

And he heard an angel sing in reply. "Thank you, Mr. Clown. I like peng'ns. My daddy and I saw them at the zoo."

Penguin listened raptly to the new voice. He knew this was his guardian angel, she who would guard and protect him forever. Sure enough, the Creator set him gently into his angel's hand. Her hands, much smaller than the Creator's—which was fitting since who among the angels had such power as the Creator?—were a bit sticky. He squealed as she held him aloft to receive the glorious light.

"Look, Daddy! It's a peng'n!"

"Yes it is, Angie. It's a very nice penguin. Did you thank the nice man for the balloon?"

Penguin wondered if the new voice belonged to another angel, but was content to bask in the warmth of his new station rather than question further the nature of the universe.

"Uh huh, I did so, didn't I, Mr. Clown?"

Penguin heard the Creator laugh. It was a wondrous sound.

"She sure did. You're very welcome, sweetie."

Penguin was waved dizzyingly around as his angel brandished him in the air.

"I got a peng'n!" his angel declared.

Penguin almost swooned from rapture.

"Come along, Angie, you're holding up the line."

"Okay, Daddy."

A rush of air pushed against Penguin's head, threatening to tear him out of his angel's hands. He felt her grip him, clutching him with her sticky fingers.

Penguin did not understand what came next. Winds blinded him and sounds assailed him, but he did not fear. He peered up into the face of his angel, dazzled by the flash and glitter of the sun as it played over her hair. His golden-haired angel beamed back at him, and he knew he was safe.

WHEN HE BECAME aware again of his surroundings, all was quiet. He rested in a beam of warmth in the center of a shadowed plain. His angel was nowhere to be seen.

"Hey!"

Penguin started in surprise. Who had addressed him?

"Hello?" he said.

"Over here, dude. I'm Ducky."

Penguin peered around until he spied a dirty lump of yellow. A jagged black rift split one side of it open, while dirt and mud coated it in a dusting of filth. He could barely make out the blunt bill and black eyes of the misshapen creature.

"Oh. Hello there," he said. "I'm Penguin."

"Yeah, hi," Ducky said. "Salutations and all that. But hey, I don't got a lot of time, so listen up. Seeing as you're new here, I just wanted to give you a heads-up and welcome you to the pit. Quick bit of advice: keep your beak down, and just run with it, no matter how bad it gets. Eventually the little demon gets distracted."

"Demon?" Penguin asked. "What do you mean?"

"Y'know. The kid. The one that brought you in."

"You mean my angel?"

Ducky laughed; it was a coarse, rasping sound. "She ain't no angel. Who do you think did all this?"

Penguin looked past Ducky into the shadows.

Around him spread a panorama of suffering.

Penguin stood amongst a litter of wretched creatures in various attitudes of ruin. On its side, a periwinkle rabbit sprawled, blind and tattered. Two long, pink ears twisted in a stranglehold around a face worn smooth of features. Beside it, a bright green froggy hung out of a lemon-yellow box. Bits of white plastic spine glinted from its torn back. An unidentifiable shape listed in the corner; its body was a shapeless mound of brown. A crooked paw jerked in a parody of a friendly wave.

Penguin gasped and averted his eyes.

"She took out my pal, the Bunster, last week," Ducky continued. "And just this morning she tore up butterfly-wings over there." He nodded in the direction of the window. Gleaming in a frilly violet dress, a delicate fairy hung in front of the pane of glass, depending from a length of purple yarn. Her eyes were closed and she seemed to be asleep.

"Hey, babe, turn around so the new guy can take a gander at what happened to you."

The fairy's eyes snapped wide and she glowered at Ducky. She reached behind her body. A soft ticking began in her chest. Her tiny feet beat against the air and she twirled around on her bit of yarn. Like burned cloth unfolding, Penguin saw the tattered remnants of the fairy's wings. A gash traveled halfway across the gossamer lavender and cream membranes draped across her back. The ragged edges looked ugly and uneven. A shiny silver key protruded from between them. Its smooth shape stood out against the wreckage.

Penguin gulped. "What happened?"

"The kid thought she was 'pretty,'" Ducky said.

Penguin shook his head; squeaks of dismay issued

from him. "No! My angel is a creature of mercy."

"Believe what you like, dude. I—" Ducky's voice stopped mid-sentence as though the words had been turned off in his throat.

"Bath time!"

It was a new voice, one Penguin hadn't heard before.

"I don't wanna bath, Mommy."

"You never do, but you have to have one. You're all dirty from the zoo."

"I don't wanna!"

The other voice sighed. "Angie, do we have to do this *every* night? Here, take your rubber ducky."

Ducky was hoisted into the ether. Penguin heard him whisper "Oh, crud" before he disappeared from sight.

"Yuck, how did this thing get so dirty?" the other voice asked.

"I want my ducky!"

"Hang on, let me clean him off."

"Nooo!" Ducky's wail was long and dismayed.

His angel and the other voice drifted away, taking Ducky with them. Penguin felt very confused.

If what Ducky said was right, the Creator had doomed him to an existence fraught with peril and suffering at the hands of a fiend. But that made no sense. Why would the Creator—the all-knowing, breath-of-life-giving creator of the universe—do such a thing? Penguin shook his head. No, Ducky must be wrong.

He sneaked a glance at the fairy. She hung in the window, shifting lightly in the breeze. Her ruined wings hung from her shoulders and her face was blank.

The only way that Penguin could reconcile what he knew was right—that the Creator was kind and good—with what he saw before him, was that the world had to be as good as it was possible for it to be. The Creator made goodness, so therefore, this world, even with the suffering and pain in it, must be the best world there could possibly be.

Penguin nodded to himself. Yes, that was the answer.

It wasn't until much later that Ducky returned. He was cleaner now, but the lack of grime coating his body highlighted the scarring on his yellow body. One of his little black eyes was half worn away.

"Hello," Penguin said.

Ducky just stared at him without speaking.

"I've figured it out," Penguin continued. He was quite excited to be able to share his realization with his new friend. "This is the best possible world!"

Ducky continued not to speak.

"It's the only answer. The Creator is a kindly being, and his angels are creatures of mercy and compassion. Therefore, what my angel does, she does for the sake of mercy."

"You. Are. Insane." Ducky's voice sounded strangled. He gave a great cough and spat gray, cloudy liquid from his beak. He vomited up the murky fluid and it poured from his bill and from the tear in his side.

"What happened?" Penguin asked, alarmed.

"They bleached me," Ducky said, sputtering up a few more drops of dirty water. "And I *still* had to do bath time."

"I'm sorry," Penguin said. "But it was the best of all things." He wanted his friend to see the truth of it.

Ducky rolled his one good eye. "I can tell you for sure, it wasn't no best of nothing."

"It has to be. You just don't understand."

Ducky shook his head. "Is what happened to butterfly-wings over there for the best?"

"Yes! It has to be."

"Dude. The Creator, if there is such a guy, ain't no good ole boy. He's a cruel s.o.b. that gets his jollies from watching us simple folks squirm. Or else there's no 'Creator,' which is what I'm figuring."

"Of course there's a Creator," Penguin said. "He made me. He made you. If there wasn't a Creator, we wouldn't be here to discuss it."

"Whatever, dude. I just know this life's rough and we gotta stick together if we want to get by. At the end of it all, there's a long drive to the dump."

"Don't you believe in anything?"

"Nope. Just in me, the Duckster."

Penguin thought that was very sad. But before he could argue his case, he was interrupted by the voice of his angel.

"Where's my peng'n?"

She was calling for him.

"Honey, you can't go to bed with a balloon." It was the voice Penguin had first heard with his angel, the one called "Daddy."

"I want my peng'n, Daddy."

"Honey—"

"Now!"

The voice sighed. "Fine. But if you pop it, don't come crying to me."

Daddy lifted Penguin from his perch.

"Hang in there, buddy! Just go with it," Ducky called after him.

Penguin was set into his angel's hands. They were no longer sticky.

"My peng'n!"

He felt a great pressure in his head as his angel squeezed his feet. His beak expanded to twice its normal size, and then three times as the breath of the Creator was forced from his base up into his head. The pain was unlike anything he had experienced before, like his very skin would rupture from the strain of too much breath-of-the-Creator. He squeaked in distress, squealing in his angel's hands.

"Angie, I told you, if you squeeze your penguin, he'll pop."

"My peng'n!" his angel shouted.

The pressure let up from his beak and he grew light-headed. The world spun around as his angel swung him in wild arcs, back and forth. He struck something and the concussion pushed the white plaiting of his belly out of alignment. A scream shrilled out of him.

He heard a wet honk.

His angel released him and he shot out of her hands and drifted to the carpet.

"It's my ducky!" his angel said. Dazed and still in pain, Penguin looked down. His angel now had Ducky in her hands and was banging him against the wall. Each time he contacted the hard, pink surface, Ducky gave a whooshing squawk of pain.

"If you don't settle down, I won't read you a bedtime story. Don't you want a bedtime story?"

Ducky fell to the floor, dropped precipitously. He tumbled and came to a stop beside Penguin.

"You...okay...dude?" Ducky gasped.

"You saved me," Penguin said.

"Yep. Told ya, I believe in me, the Duckster. And the Duckster don't let newbies get the stuffing beat out of them their first night here." Ducky coughed. "Tomorrow night, you're on your own."

Penguin didn't know what to say; he was so grateful. Before he could find the right words, Ducky shrieked. A great foot had planted itself squarely on Ducky's belly, pushing it almost to the ground. The gash in Ducky's side tore wider until it nearly split him in two. Ducky's eyes widened as he screamed out his life.

"Dammit."

Penguin watched large hands lift Ducky. They turned Ducky around and upside down.

"Ducky?" Penguin called. "Are you hurt?"

Ducky gave no reply.

"I think this thing is broken for good."

"You broke my ducky?" Penguin's angel said.

"I'm sorry, honey. He was broken already, but I think he's done for good now. We'll buy you a better ducky tomorrow, okay?"

His angel pondered this for a moment and then smiled widely. "I get a new ducky tomorrow?"

Penguin watched, stunned, as Daddy took Ducky away. He had no choice but to listen when Daddy came back and told a tale about three pigs and a destructive wolf.

Later that night, after his angel had fallen asleep and Daddy had put Penguin back in his place, Penguin thought about what had happened this day—how he had been born into glory at the Creator's hands, of his angel meting out pain, and of Ducky's sacrifice and death. It just didn't make sense.

Was the Creator cruel and capricious like Ducky

had said? Or was he kindly and benevolent, making the best of all possible worlds and gifting his creations thereby with it? Penguin wasn't sure. He sat there thinking about it all night long until dawn's amber-tinged rays washed over him through the nursery window.

Penguin looked up in surprise, still no closer to understanding the nature of the universe, but shaken out of his reverie by the light. He saw the fairy. She flinched and made a small sound when the wind blowing through the open window spun her around in a twisting corkscrew. Her eyes were shut but Penguin didn't think she was asleep.

"Fairy?" Penguin called.

She twitched and her eyes blinked open. "What?"

"Are you all right?"

The fairy glared at Penguin but after a moment her expression softened.

"Yeah. I guess so." She shrugged and her ruined wings crackled behind her. "I was trying to go back to sleep. I want to lose myself again."

"Lose yourself?"

"Yeah." A wisp of smile curved the fairy's mouth. It withered away a moment later. "The Daddy read a story to that *creature* once about a land where magical people fly on the wind and see the world as a great tapestry beneath them. They watch over it but don't ever land because then they'd have to stay. It was a dumb story." She flicked a hand dismissively. "But I liked it. I close my eyes and think about what it'd be like to fly high over everything—higher than the treetops, higher than anything. That way I can dream about it and forget." She frowned at Penguin. "Until someone calls me back."

"Oh," Penguin said. "I'm sorry."

The fairy relented. "Ah, don't worry about it." She tilted her head and squinted down. "Hey, you look different today."

"I do?"

"Yeah, sorta skinnier. And your beak is longer."

Penguin looked himself over. She was right. His flesh wasn't as taut as when the Creator had first tied him. And he realized that his center knot, the connection that was the core of his body, was looser. Even as he thought this, he realized that the Creator's breath-of-life was escaping from him, slowly and steadily.

"I'm leaking!" he said, shocked. How could this be? He was defective. But why would the Creator make him flawed?

The fairy looked down at him, a blend of pity and sorrow on her face. "Apparently, penguins are frailer even than fairies."

Penguin tried to hold his breath, but the Creator's air continued to seep out of him.

"Fairy! What am I going to do?"

The fairy shook her head. "You're going to die, Penguin. Like the rest of us."

"But I don't want to die!"

"No one does. But we all do."

"Help me," Penguin begged. "Please."

She looked away from him, her eyes drifting to the window. Penguin followed her gaze. In a whirlwind of gold and crimson, fallen leaves whipped past the glass. Beyond the violent gale of moving color, the sun was a gleaming china plate on a bright blue tablecloth.

"Sometimes," she whispered, "sometimes it's not

easy to live." She strained her arms behind her back and tugged on the silver key. It cranked around once, twice. Twisting and spinning, she convulsed on the end of the strand of purple yarn in a frenzied dance. Her movements grew more frantic until the yarn split, and Penguin watched as the fairy plummeted down. She fell hard, sprawling before him, but she pirouetted sharply back to her feet. An arrhythmic clicking noise emerged from deep in her chest.

"What are you doing?" Penguin said.

She gyrated beside him and wrapped her slender arms around his body. "I'm helping you." Her wings unfolded in a web of torn translucence. "I'm helping both of us."

With a great jeté, she flung herself into the air, carrying Penguin with her toward the open window.

At first Penguin was exhilarated at their flight and the sensation of weightlessness. The fairy held him so tightly he squeaked, but he didn't mind. The window grew large before them, the expanse of open air close enough to touch.

"We're almost through!" he squealed.

A cold wind gusted through the window, pushing them down and backwards. Penguin felt the fairy falter. He cried out as they tipped and the floor loomed close. The fairy's wings thrashed in a discordant sweep behind her. The noise in her chest spluttered and stopped altogether. Penguin thought they would be dashed back down for sure, but he felt a great push as she thrust him ahead. The fairy fell, but Penguin crested the open window. And the breeze, instead of pitching him into the nursery, lifted him away. He turned to look back at the fairy and saw her, crumpled and broken on the floor.

"Fairy!" he cried.

She lifted her head and Penguin saw her raise an arm and wave once at him through the glass. A trick of the air brought her words to him.

"Live, Penguin," she called. "Live!"

The wind tore Penguin away from the window and carried him into the sky so that he could no longer see her. Beneath him, the home of his angel wheeled away in a blur of whiteness. He spun around, helpless to control his flight. The breeze drove him higher, tumbling him beak over feet. He wished, sadly, that the fairy had made it out too.

Around him, the crackle of brilliantly hued leaves swirled in a wild dance of color. He marveled at their incredible beauty—somber green bleeding into vibrant yellows and brilliant oranges. The colors were so rich, they made him gasp with pleasure. And gasping, he realized the air was leaking faster out of him. The cold air and the
buffeting were making it worse.

But, surprising himself, Penguin found he didn't care anymore. The panic, the fear, they were gone. There was too much to see to be afraid, too much to experience to worry about dying. He whispered a quiet "thank you" to the fairy for the gift she had given him.

The leaves whisked away as though they teased him, bobbing in and out of his line of view. In a sweeping breath, they tumbled aside to reveal the land beneath. An expanse of green and gold and brown spread before him in a riotous display of color. Penguin stared. He had never seen anything so magnificent.

The wind cartwheeled him around and he found

himself staring into the brilliance of the early morning sun. Azure sky spread endlessly before him, embracing him in a bubble of infinity. He found himself spun around and around in a chaotic spiral so he wasn't sure which way was up or down anymore. He laughed aloud, happy to let the fierce and capricious breeze take him where it would.

Maybe the world wasn't as good as it should be. There was cruelty in it, and suffering. And life was short—far shorter than was fair. The wind steadied him and he found himself peering down once again at the colorscape spreading beneath him. But here and now, it was perfect. And really, there was nothing more important than that.

Penguin felt the wind racing over his rapidly shrinking body and he tasted the bright savor of the air as it shrieked by him. Not much time left. He would have liked to have flown on the wind forever and forever, just like this, but there was barely enough air left in him to hold his shape.

"I'm alive," he whispered. And as the last breath-of-the-Creator emptied out of him, he cried it out to the listening leaves and the roaring wind with all his strength. "I'm Penguin!" he shouted.

And the wind swept away the wisp of shriveled, knotted-together speck of black, orange, and white.

I wrote "The Life and Times of Penguin" after receiving a balloon animal penguin at a convention. After witnessing it come into existence at the hands of a skilled balloon artist and carefully conveying it home, I watched it slowly shrivel and deflate over the course of a couple weeks. Put me in something of an existential mood. This story is both a tribute to that short-lived balloon penguin and my homage to Voltaire's Candide. The podcast production, published by Escape Pod, *was nominated for a 2006 Parsec Award in the Best Speculative Fiction Story (short form) category.*

RUNNING ON TWO LEGS

MY MOTHER USED to tell stories of how I talked to animals when I was a little girl. And then she'd laugh when she described how indignant I got because no one believed they talked back.

I don't remember much of that period of my life. There were a lot of hospitals—white rooms, other pale children next to me, all of us with clear IV tubes taped to our parchment paper skin—and doctors, smiling men with haunted eyes that they tried so hard to keep us from seeing. That's mostly what I remember.

And then came the miraculous words "in remission." I remember those, and the tears on my mother's face when the doctor said them, for once without the not-quite-hidden anguish in his eyes. Everything was better after that. After those words I remember summer days spent grubby and exhausted in the old abandoned shack behind our house. No longer did I keep company with hospital wraiths, but rather with neighborhood kids who had experienced no greater hurt than a scraped knee or a bruised shin; kids who'd never had to listen to their parents sob just outside their door, thinking you couldn't hear them; and kids who had no memory of being so sick that even the feel of a blanket was unbearable agony.

I think I stopped talking to animals then. Or maybe I just had better things to do than listen to the birds chattering at my window or the squirrels quarrelling in the tree outside.

But I heard them again today.

"Man chicks pelted my nest," I heard through the rolled-down window of our old Honda Civic as we pulled into the parking lot of the clinic.

"Did you say something?" I asked my husband.

Kevin shook his head. He needed a haircut. The waves in his hair were turning into frizzy curls in the Georgia heat. I mourned the Civic's air conditioner, its cooling breeze a memory of more prosperous days.

"Time to build again," I heard. And I recognized the voice—a shrill, helium babble, a tone I hadn't heard in over two decades. I looked up, and sure enough, I saw the muted berry-red breast of a she-robin hopping on a branch beside the tattered remains of a nest. Another bird, a brown one with white shoulders, cocked its head sympathetically.

That's when I knew. Even before I saw the doctor—a woman this time, but still with the same cheery smile that couldn't conceal the sorrow that was a requisite of her job—I knew.

Kevin held my hand in reception as we waited to be called. They didn't keep us stewing for long. Maybe when the results are bad, they try to cut you a break on the limbo time spent half bored, half terrified amongst the screaming children and the old issues of *People* and *National Geographic*.

Dr. Graykin didn't bother with small talk; she never did. "The results of your biopsy came back, Ginny. I'm afraid it's not good. The tests showed a malignancy."

I expected to feel horrified, or at the very least, afraid. But instead, all I could think of were the words of the robin. "Time to build again." How did birds mark time?

It was Kevin who reacted. "Cancer?" The word was a gasp, a choked whisper.

"I'm afraid so."

"What are our options?" he said.

Our options. Sometimes I got mad at Kevin when he inadvertently left my name off memberships he signed us up for—like the Paperback Book club, or the Music of the Month club. For that matter, the cable was still only in his name. But he remembered this time.

"I'd recommend a rigorous course of chemotherapy," Dr. Graykin said. "I'm afraid this is a fairly aggressive form of cancer. And because of the nature of the tumor, I believe a hysterectomy will be necessary. The last set of x-rays showed another mass already forming. Complete removal of the impacted organs will give us the best chance of beating this."

Now Dr. Graykin was included in my prognosis. Give *us* the best chance, she'd said.

"What are my odds?" With that one word: *my*, I let the illusion slip. It crumbled to dust like brittle flower husks in winter, exposing me to what the doctor and my husband had been trying to shield me from. But this was my fight and my sickness, mine and mine alone. In the end, it'd be me vomiting my insides out from the chemo, too weak to even raise a hand to brush the hair out of my eyes. No matter how supportive Kevin was, or how solicitous Dr. Graykin, they couldn't carry that for me.

"I'd say pretty good," Dr. Graykin said. "I think we've caught it early enough. Maybe seven out of ten women can expect to push it into remission, assuming you act decisively now."

Seven out of ten. My future was laid out, reduced to a number game of statistics and uncertainty.

I let Kevin make the follow-up appointments with the receptionist, scheduling when I would have the poisons pumped into my veins to kill the cells that had turned against me, setting the date for when they'd excise the organs that were killing me like Trojan horse invaders from the inside.

Back in the car, I sat listening to the birds.

"Wind's changing. Thunderstorm flying in on cloud wings," I heard.

I'd never learned what the birds indigenous to Georgia were, their feather patterns or migratory habits. But I knew what this one would look like from his voice. He'd be one of those little brownish-gray birds that dive at crows to scare them away from their nests. It always impressed me how fearless they were, attacking other birds that were two, sometimes three times larger.

Kevin stared into space behind the wheel. The keys dangled from his fingers, idle.

"Rain shoos worms out," the bird said.

"We'll get through this," Kevin finally said. "But no kids on top of everything else—"

His words dribbled away, and between us, silence dug its fingernails in.

No kids. After the hysterectomy I wouldn't be able to experience the wonder of growing a new life inside of me. I'd never feel a tiny person develop within me nor go through the process of expelling it forth in a gush of agony and hope. I wondered why I didn't grieve, why I didn't mourn for the children of my womb that I'd never have. But I felt distant, detached.

"Full gullet follows the rains," the bird chirped.

The Civic's motor revved as Kevin turned the key in the ignition, drowning out the bird's voice.

At home, Kevin fidgeted. I felt sorry for him. He didn't know what to do with himself. I wasn't reacting the way the tragedy-struck heroines on television did; I wasn't crying or shouting or throwing things. He was waiting to be my rock, my solace, and I just sat in the kitchen, staring out the window.

"You should go back to work," I said.

"I can't leave you alone at a time like this."

"We can't afford for you to lose your job." The words *and your health insurance* were left unspoken, but I knew both of us were thinking them. "I'll be fine."

I felt him at my shoulder, reaching out to comfort me. "You sure?"

I moved away, knew it when his hand fell back. "It's just cancer. I beat the odds once. I can do it again."

It was false bravado, but Kevin needed to hear it. It allowed him to gather up his briefcase and his keys and drive away from me.

And besides, I really wasn't alone. I waited until I could no longer hear our old car sputtering down the road before I went out to the host of voices I knew were in our backyard.

Our yard is large and fenced in. I think the

previous owners had a dog. The fence is old and there are gaps in it large enough to admit cats, rabbits, squirrels, and once I saw a raccoon from the kitchen window. It's an unkempt area, our big backyard. Neither Kevin nor I enjoy yard work and the weeds had grown roughshod through the grass. Unidentifiable greenery sprouted tiny white flowers, like miniature daisies, cascading over a failing landscaped bush that sagged from the invader's weight. Thin, tall trees—fruit trees, evergreens, and shrubs—shaded the far corner; long-dead tree trunks intermingled with the quick. The evergreens spewed a profusion of pinecones year round, making mowing a risk-fraught undertaking; the flora itself endorsed our laissez-faire grounds keeping.

I sat on the old wooden bench; its white paint, slashed into streamers by time, revealed the dry, cracked wood beneath, and I listened.

"Got a seed? Got a seed?" trilled from the leaf-canopy overhead.

"Sky fly high."

"The sun. Lookit the sun!"

Then I heard a non-avian speaker. "Wanna bite," it said. It was a nasal voice; it reminded me of a young Jimmy Durante.

"No bite." That voice also had a nasal drone to it, but it was seasoned by maturity.

Out of the cover of a riotously blooming weed-shrub, a soft-furred black face pushed through, crowned with a cap of white. Small black ears and India-ink eyes swiveled to regard me. A round barrel body with two broad, white stripes down the back trundled out. Behind her, a miniature copy tagged at her heels. The ripe aroma of unwashed socks wafted over me.

They say that a skunk out during the day must be rabid, but I knew these two weren't. Rabid animals don't exude patient resignation, or, in the case of Junior, unbridled elation. Another urban wilderness myth debunked, I guess.

Mama Skunk trotted up to me, the size of a small housecat but with that sweeping tail no cat possessed. I breathed through my mouth and hoped that Junior wasn't trigger-happy. Mama didn't seem to notice my poised anxiety, or if she did, she didn't comment on it.

"Wanna bite," Junior said.

"No bite," Mama repeated. She sat down, not two steps from my bench; her hind legs sprawled out on either side of her.

I began to relax. The smell, though not agreeable, wasn't aggressively offensive, not much worse than a rain-drenched German Shepherd.

With great dignity, she scratched at a spot behind her

ear—one hind leg a blur of movement. "Teeth on this one comin' in," she said. "Needs to set 'em in everything he sniffs."

To illustrate, Junior launched himself at Mama's hindquarters and sunk his gleaming white teeth into her haunches.

Mama gave a weary sigh. "Small ones." While Junior worried at her, she gazed up at me. "Third of the year, he is. First daughter and second and fourth sons crushed by four-wheels on the road."

"I'm sorry."

She swiped at Junior with a paw. It dislodged him momentarily. "My second breeding season. First was an only daughter. Owl took her. Takes a lot out, raising small ones and watching them die."

"I'm sorry," I repeated. I wasn't sure what else to say.

"One more season in me, I think. Then I'm done. No more egg crunch in my teeth or juicy caterpillar fur sticky on my tongue." She hissed at Junior as he dug his baby fangs into her leg. "No bite!"

"Wanna bite."

Mama snatched Junior up by the scruff of his neck and snapped her head sharply to the side. "No bite!"

"No bite," Junior squeaked, hanging from her mouth.

Mama released him and Junior sprang at her back, chewing at the thick fur there. She nodded to me, a single bob of her nose, and turned to go. Junior tumbled off in a sprawl of oversized paws and bushy tail, and scampered after her.

"If small ones could bite the moon, they would," she called over her shoulder. "But no one wants a chewed-up moon."

Bemused, I watched them flatten themselves under my fence, the flags of their tails disappearing beneath it. I made a mental note to put out a tray of snacks—leftovers from dinner, perhaps—for Mama and Junior tonight.

A flash of violet caught my eye as a blue jay fluttered onto one of our wild cherry trees. "Beware the wind!" he called.

"I'm watching. I'm watching," another voice replied.

I scanned the branches but couldn't see this newcomer. From the sharpness of the tone, I was betting it was a woodpecker, but wasn't sure.

"Won't rustle my nest," the maybe-woodpecker chirped. "Go fly."

The blue jay flitted away.

"Gotta build for a storm," the unseen bird said. "But sometimes blown down anyway. The sun's out now. Lookit! Lookit!"

Another voice joined in and a chorus of "Lookit"s ensued.

I listened to the birds discuss the weather until the labored engine of the Civic announced my husband's return.

Kevin tossed his briefcase into a chair and his keys onto the table as I started some rice boiling for dinner.

"I sat in the backyard this afternoon," I said. "I've decided I like the overgrown look. Some of the weeds are prettier than the landscaped flowers."

"I can get the mower out of the tool shed this weekend."

"No, I'm serious. I like it." I rinsed off a stalk of bok choy and began chopping it into chunks. The stem and the browning parts I deposited into a bowl. Mama and Junior Skunk would appreciate the tidbits.

"Ginny, did you call my folks with the news yet?"

I tossed a bundle of bean sprouts into the strainer and sent a cascade of water over them. "No. I don't really know what to say to them." I picked out several choice sprouts and set them in the same bowl as the bok choy stem.

"Want me to do it?"

I didn't look up from the carrots and parsnips on the cutting board. "Would you?" I made it a game, seeing how evenly I could chop them.

While Kevin dialed, I poured oil into the wok and

dropped in some diced green onion and teriyaki sauce to simmer.

Outside, I saw wings flash in the treetops.

"Hi, Mom. Ginny and I got word back from her biopsy

today—"

I concentrated on making dinner: mushrooms for us, mushrooms in the skunk bowl, eggplant for us, eggplant in the bowl.

Even across the room, with the headset against Kevin's ear, I could hear his mother sobbing. Part of it, most of it probably, was for me. But I was sure a little bit was for them too. From the moment we'd announced our engagement, his parents, especially his mother, had talked about grandchildren. I felt like I was shirking them by having Kevin break the bad news, but on the other hand, I knew the phone call would be good for him. His mother was reacting the way I should have, dissolving into tears and railing at fate. He spoke in soothing tones, the epitome of tender consolation. It gave him something to focus on, something to do.

The tang of cooking bell peppers suffused with curry and cinnamon drifted from the wok and permeated the kitchen. I dumped in the sprouts and turned down the heat.

"Dinner's just about ready," I said.

Kevin nodded and began the process of extracting himself from the phone. He was reluctant, but I heard him address his father. Undoubtedly my dad-in-law had taken over comforting Kevin's mother.

I poured us some iced tea out of the refrigerator as he replaced the headset onto the cradle.

Kevin watched me eat; I could feel his eyes, over

the bottle of soy sauce, following me as I forked up mouthfuls of rice and vegetables.

"I spent today thinking," I said.

Kevin put down his fork, his food untouched. "About what?"

I'd forgotten to toss some peanuts into the stir-fry. Peanuts were one of Kevin's favorites. "The chemotherapy, the surgery," I said. "I remember what chemo was like when I was a kid. I remember thinking that letting the leukemia have me would've been better."

The silence stretched. The sound of my own teeth crunching through celery and carrots was deafening.

"Did you ever think how unnatural it is, going through all that medical rigmarole to extend our lives?" I continued. "When wild animals get sick, they don't stress it, don't claw for those extra few weeks or months or years. They just accept it. Maybe it's better that way."

Kevin made a sound; I don't think it was a word. He stared at me, and I had to look away. I couldn't handle the confused hurt, stark on his face, that I'd glimpsed.

I stood up with my half-eaten plate of food and dumped it and the bowl of vegetable leavings onto a plate. The back door's unoiled hinges creaked as I wrenched it open.

Kevin didn't follow me. I hadn't expected him to.

I'd just unlatched the screen door when I heard the scream.

"No! Not me! Aii!"

I rushed out and saw a calico tabby cat examining a tuft of gray fur between its paws. I recognized the cat as one of the strays that roamed the neighborhood from the jagged scar across its nose. As I watched, the cat opened the trap of its claws and the animal leapt free. It was tiny—a mouse, or a vole maybe.

"Run," the cat growled.

The terrified little creature scampered towards me. I didn't think it was seeking me out; it was just running away from the cat. It screamed, high pitched and inarticulate.

I took a step forward but the cat was faster. It pounced and the tiny animal's screams ended, cut off. I heard the snap of fragile bones shattering between sharp teeth.

My headlong rush petered out before the momentum could build beyond the first adrenalin jolt. It had all happened too quickly.

The tabby spat out the mouse-vole and prodded the now-limp body. His golden eyes gleamed in the twilight. "Fought well, small warm fur," he said. "Tried to bite me. Such small fangs. Mine are much finer." He shook his paws at the dead rodent and turned his back to it. "It's still now."

"Aren't you at least going to eat it?" I said.

The cat's tail flicked back and forth like a plump, furry serpent. "Not hungry."

"Then why'd you kill it if you aren't going to eat it?" Indignation made my voice harsh.

Yellow-slitted eyes met mine. "It was there."

Before I could reply, he bounded across my yard, scaled the fence in a single prodigious leap, and was gone.

I set the plate of food down, half surprised to still find it in my hands, and went over to the pathetic corpse in the overgrown grass. A trickle of blood spattered a soft-muzzled face, plastering the fur around its head and neck. It was still warm. I wondered if I ought to bury it.

Still undecided, I stood up. Movement from above caught my attention. Against the shading of the darkening lavender sky, I saw silhouettes flit and flutter. Voices drifted to me, excited and high-pitched.

"There!"

"Caught it."

"Mine."

"Listen."

Bats. Little brown ones out in the dusk, hunting insects. Such chaotic energy, a wild dance in the sky. And not once did a dancer misstep; they all seemed to know the exact cadence and meter of their frenetic waltz. I watched them dive and careen above me until it grew too dark to see.

"Warm blood is sweeter, but tonight it is cold." The speaker's voice was precise, a softly calculating presence. An owl.

I wouldn't have to dig a grave for the tiny dead thing in my yard. I retreated, returning to the voice-free refuge of my kitchen.

It was deserted.

The door to Kevin's den was closed, but when I knocked on it, the knob turned and the door swung open as though he'd been waiting for me.

He hadn't changed out of his work clothes; his shirt was wrinkled and his tie loose and askew around his neck. I couldn't meet his eyes—familiar soft blue eyes that crinkled in laughter at our private jokes, ones that no one else would understand. Those eyes would hold anguish, I knew, pain I had caused. There might be tears in them if I looked up. I stared at his chin.

"I didn't write down when my appointments were," I said. "Do you still have the cards the receptionist gave you?"

I let myself peek after all. Yes, blue eyes the color of the evening sky, still pained, but also relieved. I'd given him back something to hope for.

I AVOIDED THE outdoors after that. I kept the windows closed and the radio or television, or both, turned up to drown out even the hint of wilderness voices. Trips to the hospital for the start of my chemotherapy were made with the car radio blaring and culminated in a hasty, unseeing, unhearing dash from parking lot to foyer.

The drugs made me tired and everything I ate became seasoned by flakes of rust. But the hint of nausea I felt when I watched the clear solution dripping into my arm during the first treatment didn't manifest beyond a suggestion of misery. I was thankful for that.

Days disappeared, unmarked and unremembered while the poisons did their work. Then came the one scribbled on my calendar by Kevin, like a birthday or anniversary.

He drove us to the hospital and hovered nearby as the nurses and interns took charge of me. In hospitals, nobody's clothing fits properly. Doctors flurried by, the wings of their white lab coats and smocks loose in their wakes. Fellow patients slouched or reclined under a stratum of blankets and hospital gowns. And my attendants' slate blue scrubs transformed them into anonymous, androgynous drones that buzzed and twittered about me. When they donned their facemasks, the illusion was complete—featureless, genderless eunuchs, all of them. In my baggy hospital garb, I joined their fellowship. But they could take off their uniforms and become people again. I, on the other hand, would be a true eunuch after today, hollowed out and sterile.

I watched as one of them tightened a tourniquet on my arm and slid a shining needle into the faintly pulsing vein in the crook of my elbow. I dutifully counted down from ten, and embraced the darkness that crowded the edges of the room when I hit four.

Three. Two. One.

SOMEONE HAD ERECTED a nest of cotton balls and gauze in my mouth and hastily dismantled it while I slept. I was left with the taste of desiccated foundation.

I opened my eyes and immediately closed them again. Surely the world was not supposed to be a dizzying slash of color and light?

"Ginny?" I recognized Kevin's voice. "I saw her open her eyes, doctor."

"She should be coming out of the anesthesia," Dr. Graykin said. "It can be disorienting."

I remembered now. I had been un-womaned in the limbo of three numbers, carved up and sewn back together again. "I'm awake," I said. Although it didn't sound right, more like "Mm, wwm." I tried again. "I'm here." I squinted my eyes open, relieved to discover that the room wasn't still canting sideways.

I felt Kevin's fingers against my hand, felt the brush of his lips on my forehead. "How're you feeling?"

"I wouldn't nominate today as one of my all-time

favorites," I mumbled.

"You'll probably be sore for a while," Dr. Graykin said. "A week, at least. You'll need to take it very easy."

I had been blissfully oblivious of my body until I heard the word *sore*. Then I became aware of a deep ache running through me. Each breath pulled at low parts of me that were unhappy and eager to complain. My arm throbbed where the IV line punctured it, tethering me to a jellyfish-flaccid bag.

"The procedure went smoothly," Dr. Graykin continued. "We were able to visualize the tumor in its entirety."

"Oh. Good."

"You should rest now. Let the nurse on duty know if you need anything." Dr. Graykin patted my sheet-shrouded leg and was gone in a whirl of white before I could finish mouthing a thank you.

Kevin handed me a tastefully cheery, pink envelope. I produced the obligatory smile at the cuter-than-cute bunny on the cover of the card. The inside read "*Hopping* you get well soon!"

"Thanks, honey." The words sounded dismal, even to me.

Kevin leaned over and brushed his lips against my cheek.

I closed my eyes.

"Try to get some sleep. I'll see you tomorrow."

"Okay. Bye."

That night, alone in my hospital bed, I dreamed that I was Prometheus, chained to the bench in my yard while crows picked at me, tearing out my ovaries and uterus with their sharp beaks and crying "Lookit! Lookit!"

I didn't need a psychoanalyst to interpret it.

I woke with the curtains of my room just beginning to turn from a colorless gray to a pale dandelion-buff. Birds would be singing outside, announcing the dawn. I couldn't hear them, and suddenly I wanted to.

I swung my legs over the edge of my bed, careful not to tangle my IV line, and lurched the two steps to the window. My legs were uncooperative, intent upon tripping me up. The pain intensified and I staggered against the window casing. My eyes felt scalded, like a handful of salt had been tossed into them. I reached a hand up and discovered that my face was wet. Tears. Why was I crying? Weeping, standing, the window, it was too much for me to manage. My legs gave way and I crumpled, taking the metal tree that held my now-empty IV bag with me. Pain erupted through me and I couldn't stop myself from crying out.

The soft shushing of rubber-soled shoes on tile pattered to my door. The door opened; light enveloped me.

"Oh my goodness! Mrs. Broward, what are you doing?" It was the night nurse.

"The w-window," I sobbed. "I j-just wanted to open the window."

She righted the IV stand and half-lifted me to my feet. The tears wouldn't stop and each time I hiccupped, another spear of pain tore through my body. I no longer felt distressed at the closed window; I just felt ridiculous.

"There, there, Mrs. Broward." The nurse settled me back into bed, handed me a tissue, and checked my bandages.

My nose dripped disgustingly. Blowing it hurt.

"I'm sorry. I don't know what came over me."

"It's the hormones and all the stress from the operation. It's perfectly normal." She tucked the blankets in around me. "Comfy?"

I nodded. My eyelids were heavy again, weighted by hot coins.

"Right then. Just hit the red button if you need me."

"Okay," I mumbled. The nurse's face grew hazy and the edges of the room softened around me.

She patted my hand. "Henry's coming 'round today. I'll make sure he swings by here first thing. He's good at getting a grin. Smiling is its own medicine."

I don't remember her leaving. When I opened my eyes again, the curtains were a radiant canary-yellow. A hollow rapping echoed from my door. It was that sound which had awakened me.

"Come in."

The door opened a crack and a man's face peered around the edge. It was an unobtrusive face; creases at the eyes and forehead spoke of time spent in the sun. He wasn't a doctor; there was too much buoyancy in his eyes.

"Did I wake you?" he said. "Judy, the nurse, told me I should come by."

Memories of a first light conversation filtered into my consciousness. I struggled to sit up. "Are you Henry?"

The man pushed the door wide. "Actually, my name's Dave. But Henry's with me."

I heard a soft clicking, like a strand of pearls being coiled together. A tawny yellow and black, indisputably canine muzzle, poked around my door.

The head, level with Dave's thigh, was long and graceful atop a brindle-shaded neck. Bright brown eyes peered up at me while a wide mouth lolled open in a doggie smile. It was canine nails on hospital tile that had clacked and clattered so.

"This is Henry," Dave said.

"Oh." I had thought that Henry would be a therapist or a psychiatrist.

"You're not allergic or anything, are you?" Dave said.

"No. Not at all."

Henry's ears flipped forward. "Hi," he said. "Pleased to meetcha. Very happy to. Yup."

"Henry's a greyhound rescue from a track in Florida," Dave said. He didn't react to Henry's words, but then I hadn't expected him to. "We visit the hospital every Wednesday. Judy said you needed some company?"

"Come in."

Dave led Henry to the side of my bed. I noticed something. "Hey, you've only got three legs."

"I know. I know," Henry said. "My leg was sick. They cut it off."

"Bone cancer," Dave said. "We caught it in time, but that was pretty much the end of his racing days."

"Good as new. Better. Better," Henry said. "Doesn't hurt. Can't race as fast as I used to. Boy, I really could go when I was a pup, but I can still get the wind buzzing through my ears. I like running. I'd run with two legs if I had to. Sorry. No offense."

I smiled. The curve of my lips felt alien to me, like I hadn't smiled in a very long time. I reached out to stroke the dog's head. His short fur was warm, like thick velvet beneath my fingers.

"Pet my ears," he said. "My ears. Everyone likes my ears."

So I stroked the felt and sateen of his pale yellow ears.

"Y'know," he said. "Listen up here. Listen. It doesn't matter how many legs you got. The important thing is the running. That's what I always say."

It was soothing, just petting Henry. Some of the tension, a bit of the anxiety, leaked away as I ran my fingers through his coat.

Dave ruffled the dog's head. "Hey, I have to take Henry to the kid's ward now. He's got a date with a certain little boy who's very punctuality oriented. If you like, I can swing by afterwards. Maybe let you and Henry have some quality one-on-one time?"

"That's not necessary. My husband will be in soon to take me home. But I'm glad you both came by." I gave Henry a last pat. "Thank you, Henry."

"My pleasure. You're welcome. Any time."

"And you too, Dave."

"Hey, I'm just the transportation. I know who the real star of the show is." Dave grinned down at the dog. "Ready to go, fellah? Rickie's waiting for you."

"Yeah. Yeah. Gotta go see Rickie. Yup," Henry said. "Nice to metcha, lady. Glad to make your acquaintance. See you around."

Kevin arrived while the day nurse—a slender, pinch-faced woman with brusque manners but a soothing voice—was serving me a tray of red Jell-o, oatmeal, and toast.

I pushed the unappetizing meal away. "Hi."

"Hi back. How're you doing?"

"Not too bad," I said.

"Has Dr. Graykin been by yet?"

As though he'd conjured her, she appeared at his elbow. "Good morning, Ginny. Did you sleep okay?"

"More or less."

She performed a cursory check of my vitals—heartbeat, blood pressure, temperature—and oversaw the removal of the IV umbilicus before declaring me sound. It was such a relief feeling the plastic tube slide out of my arm. I had spent more time than anyone should have to endure, violated by a slender hose piping medicines and nutrients through my veins.

The pinched-faced nurse helped me dress into proper clothes before bundling me into a wheelchair for my exodus to the hospital's patient drive.

Kevin acted as though I was a sandcastle at high tide. He hovered over me, unhappy when I wouldn't let him bodily carry me from the car into the house. But he didn't press me either, as though he were afraid that I would melt away at a strong word.

"Do you need anything? Want me to make you a sandwich?"

"I'm not hungry."

"The doctor said you should eat something. I can heat up some soup. Maybe with some bread and butter?"

"No, really. They fed me at the hospital."

"You didn't eat it."

"Really, I'm fine. I just want to lie down."

"Of course. After we get you tucked in I can bring you something light to snack on. Maybe some fruit?"

My patience splintered. "Kevin, having my reproductive organs surgically extracted did not create a gaping hole that needs stuffing. And even if it did, I hardly think food would be an adequate substitute for what I've lost unless you were thinking of cramming that fruit into me from a different orifice than my mouth."

I pushed past him and stomped upstairs, trying not to flinch when the sudden movements caused my insides to twang and bite. I wanted to bang the bedroom door shut, but I managed to cling to the last threads of civility and merely shut it.

I barely had the strength to kick off my shoes before falling into the neatly made-up bed. The last thing I saw before my eyelids slammed shut was that the window overlooking our yard was open.

CRYING WOKE ME. At first, I thought it was Kevin, but it wasn't his throat that made those heartbroken, pitiful wails. It was dark outside, but it was only a little after noon, far too early for sunset. Somber gray clouds, heavy with rain and the promise of thunder, enveloped the horizon.

Peering out the window, I realized that the sounds were coming from the yard. Without bothering to slip my shoes on, I padded to the door. Nothing stirred inside the house as I made my way through it, blinking in the false twilight.

The grass was cool under my bare feet. Edges of crabgrass like crinkly knives slashed my ankles. I nearly tripped over a white plate, hidden by overgrown weeds. It was the licked-clean plate of food I had set out an uncountable number of days ago.

The noise was coming from the tool shed nestled in the furthest recesses of our yard where we kept the neglected lawn mower and other underutilized paraphernalia.

The door squealed as I pulled it open; the hinges

were too rust-encumbered to perform smoothly. The stench of recently-fired skunk musk assailed me. No, it wasn't a *stench*; that word didn't do it justice. Fresh skunk is a transcendental state, an experience more profound than anything encompassed by as simple a sense as smell. My eyes streaked with tears and I struggled not to retch, knowing that to do so would require me to take another breath.

Through the blur of my tear-filled eyes, I saw a small black and white bundle of fury charging me. His tail stood up straight behind him, the long hairs bristling out like a Christmas tree. He was puffed up, standing on his toes to appear as large as possible. It was Junior.

"Go 'way!" he shrilled in his Jimmy Durante voice.

"Don't shoot," I whispered, half-choked. "I'm going away, see?"

At the sound of my voice, he stopped mid-charge. His tail drooped and he deflated. "Wait. Need help," he said.

I tried breathing through my mouth, but I could still smell the musk. When I inhaled, my tongue and the back of my throat became swathed with a foul, oily coating.

"What's the matter?" I gasped.

"Mama poofed someone. I run away. She won't wake up."

"She was attacked?"

"Just here. Lookie."

A still puddle of black and white lay in the shadows. It was Mama Skunk. She was dead, her neck snapped.

"Oh, Junior, I'm so sorry. Your mother's not waking up."

Junior butted and pawed at her, whining and snuffling forlornly.

"What happened?" No sane animal would tangle with a skunk. And obviously Mama had got in a shot. For her assailant to have managed to snap her neck after being hit, I couldn't fathom it.

"Cat," Junior said. "All scarred up. No sniffer."

And I remembered the calico cat, the one that had killed the mouse-vole.

Junior's liquid black eyes gazed up at me. "Lonesome," he whimpered. "Scared." He began to cry, small snuffling noises both like and unlike a weeping human child.

"I'm sorry," I said again. The words felt inadequate. "Are you hungry? You're probably hungry. Let me get you something to eat." I reminded myself of Kevin, an uncomfortable sensation.

"Leaving me? Come back?"

"I'll be right back. Stay here."

The air was fresher outside; I inhaled with relief. The first droplets of rain plunked on my arms and shoulders.

Kevin had made soup, after all. I found a large Tupperware bowl in the refrigerator filled with some cream-based concoction. It would have milk in it, and vegetables, maybe cheese. I ladled up a bowlful and debated whether I needed to microwave it for Junior. But no, I was still inundated by the residue of Mama Skunk's last stand. The less time I spent in the house, the less exhaustive the fumigation efforts would have to be. I hoped.

I was on my way out the door when I heard Junior's screams. They were high-pitched and shrill, inhuman. The bowl shattered on the kitchen linoleum as I ran out. Tendrils of sizzling pain oscillated from my nether regions up through my chest in a pulsating rhythm. I doubted whether Dr. Graykin would classify sprinting as "taking it very easy." I caught my breath, and instantly gagged. I'd thought that the stink couldn't possibly get any worse. A fresh infusion of skunk spray proved me wrong.

I tried to ignore the raindrops now hammering down from above, but they trickled into my eyes and made the grass slick. The throbbing turned into a persistent flare of pain as I slid and stumbled through our yard. Despite the toxic miasma that hovered around the tool shed, I rushed in.

The relief from the rain vied with a wave of nausea from the redoubled aura of skunk. In the storm's gloom, the shed was pitch.

I pushed the door wide. A single strobe of lightning splashed whiteness and shadows in with the rain. In the moment of washed-out over brilliance, I saw Junior, huddled in the scant shelter of the mower where it leaned against the wall. The lightning framed the calico cat in mid-leap as it sprang.

Blinded again, but trusting in the afterimage memory, I dove.

"Don't shoot!" I shouted at Junior.

My hand closed over a screeching, furious ball of teeth and claws. The cat sank its fangs in but I didn't let go. Red-hot wires scored my wrist and I felt teeth grate against bone in my palm.

Another slash of lightning lit the shed. I wrestled the scratching, biting demon to the dust-covered crate that housed moldering copies of Kevin's old comic books and magazines. I threw the cat in, slammed the lid shut, and latched it.

My hands and arms felt like I'd set them on fire. More worrisome, I felt wetness trickling down my side through the bandages. "Junior?" I panted. "Where are you?"

"Mama?" I felt a cold nose nudge my ankle. "Mama?"

I kneeled, doing my best not to breathe, and picked Junior up with my smarting arms. "You okay?"

He immediately nestled into me, snuffling at my face. It felt good, his warm, soft body snug against me.

"Oh my God!" Kevin exclaimed behind me. I turned and was blinded by a flashlight beam.

Junior squawked and tried to burrow under my arm.

Kevin repositioned the light so it no longer blazed into my eyes. I could imagine the picture I presented. I was drenched, barefoot, my hands and arms scored and bleeding, rank with musk, and cuddling a baby skunk. But Kevin surprised me. After only the shortest of explanations, he helped me and Junior back to the house, phoned animal control to collect the cat I had trapped in the shed, and took charge of Junior, setting him up with a bowl of soup and a blanket-lined box in the spare bathroom.

"We're adopting a skunk, huh?" He got out the peroxide and began dabbing at my bites and scratches. "Y'know, if you wanted a baby substitute, I would've thought a puppy or cat or something would've been less problematic than a skunk." He glanced up at me as he said it, his tone teasing and light. When I didn't rebuff him, he smiled shyly. "So, uh, you think we can get him de-scented?"

The rueful expression on his face made me giggle.

When was the last time I had giggled? I couldn't remember. I took his fingers in mine and winced when they brushed against my wounds.

"Kevin, I'm sorry about how I've behaved," I said. "It's just, I'm so scared all the time, I don't—"

He pulled me close and rested his chin on top of my head. "I know, honey. It's okay. I'll always love you, no matter what. Kids or no kids, even if you decide you need to adopt stray skunks and get into fights with alley cats, I'll still love you."

I laughed and something rigid that I'd been holding tight inside me dissolved away. The laughter metamorphosed unexpectedly into tears, great gasping sobs that swelled until I was helpless to stop them. I felt my knees fold. I would have fallen, but Kevin caught me. He held me in his arms as I cried, stroked my hair as I wept, my body wracked with tremor after tremor. I clung to him, my rock after all.

PEOPLE LOOK AT us funny when I tell them we have a skunk living with us.

Kevin drew the line at Junior sleeping in bed with us. But when he's at work, Junior usually curls up with me on the couch for long skunk naps. He follows me around as I tend the new vegetable garden in our backyard and gets underfoot as often as he can. When the chemotherapy made my hair fall out, his antics lured me away from fixating on the freakish apparition in my mirror. And when I feel too wrung out by the drugs to get out of bed, he drags all the covers off me, puffing and straining to haul the mass of blankets away. I laugh and find I *can* get up.

The backyard has acquired some strange attraction to four-legged and feathered types. It's especially the sick or the scared or the lonely that come to me. Cats thrown out of car windows, puppies dumped by the roadside, they find their way here and tell me their stories. Sometimes the only thing I can do is make sure they don't die cold and alone. And sometimes I have the joy of watching a newly healed bird fling itself back into the sky.

Kevin is building bat houses and birdfeeders and squirrel perches for me. And he's going to tear down the tool shed and build something better, sort of a triage sanctuary for outdoor beasties to take refuge in who can't or won't come into the house.

Dr. Graykin was displeased with me for pulling my stitches, but she thinks that between the chemo and the surgery we'll get all the cancer cells. God, I hope so. But there's never any certainty in life, no guarantees, no promises. The only thing I can do is take each day as I can and do the best by it. Or, as someone once told me: "It doesn't matter how many legs you got. The important thing is the running."

"Running on Two Legs" was nominated for a 2005 British Fantasy Award in the Best Short Story category and received an honorable mention in the 4th quarter 2002 L. Ron Hubbard Writers of the Future contest. It was inspired by my first pet skunk, Hobkin, and some folks do indeed look at me funny when I tell them about having a pet skunk, even after I assure them that yes, he was descented. But most people, the

ones who share with me the conviction that a house isn't a home unless it's got someone four-legged and furry in it, just smile and let me ramble on. Hobkin *enriched my life and reminded me to run for the joy of it, lookit the magic all around us, and to laugh every day.*

BLACK SWAN, WHITE SWAN

BIRD LAKE IS named after the multitude of avian visitors that summer on the glassy waters: mallards, wood ducks, and Canada geese. But summer is half a year away and Delia looks out on forlorn blackness, devoid of a single feathered denizen. The moon, a plump gibbous whiteness, shades the lake and its border of skeleton trees a stark chiaroscuro. Around the pier, the water is a black mirror, an expanse of fathomless reflection.

Delia complements the scenery, her face carved into pallid lines by inky streamers of hair. No one knows she is there, and no one will find her for months and months. If they ever do.

"Everyone's got a story to tell." The voice is liquid light, bright and clear as rain.

"Who's there?" Delia searches the shoreline, distraught at the idea of a trespasser on her solitude. But the lakefront remains lonely and still. Even the ice crystals her words have formed, winter's white breath, hang motionless in the air.

Concentric circles lap beneath the dock's wooden planks. A swan floats out, its shining plumage driving the water's void back.

"There's a man across the way." The swan fixes Delia with polished onyx eyes. "Sometimes he's a lighthouse and sometimes he's a train, but silence doesn't scare him."

Delia stares at the luminous bird. "I don't want a lighthouse or a train," she says.

"Sometimes he's a shelter in the rain."

Delia studies the ripples that pass through the water's surface in the swan's wake.

"Don't shut the door, it puts walls around you." The swan dips its beak. "Call me the ocean, and I'll change with the moon. You look right through me, but I can see the end of the storm."

"Stop it."

"Across the way there's a man who holds questions without asking. A little peace of heart to guard with a stone wall," the swan says. "Or a piece of heart guarded by stone walls. Let me in, and we can sing for nights."

"Go away."

The swan warbles, a musical wow-wo-ou. The wild cry startles Delia, and she takes a step back. Her foot catches on a knot jutting from the weathered planks; she unbalances, arms pinwheeling. As she tips into the icy lake, the swan takes wing, arrowing into the sky with a sweep of white feathers.

Black arms fold her to a black breast; the cold locks her lungs shut as water weights her limbs. Delia fights the embrace, even as she acknowledges her relief.

WHEN DELIA OPENS her eyes, the white dazzles her, a sail of bleached feathers in a nest of silvery down.

She blinks, and the white gains outlines and edges—a pristine bed with white sheets, pale walls, and a spotless floor.

"Welcome back."

The man is a blot of shadow, cinereous dimension to subdue the light; the slide of sable hair as it brushes his shoulders fragments the whiteness into strands of gray and tan. The carmine logo on his black t-shirt splashes words so bloody Delia can't read them, instead she rests her eyes on the whiteness of his arms—an under layer of long-sleeved insulation. Even that dims the white, a thermal shirt textured with light-muting crisscrosses.

"Do you remember anything?" he asks.

"I fell in the lake." Delia's voice is a broken bell, not the honey and cream she expected. That scares her more than the strange surroundings or the strange man. Her hand flies to her throat only to be stayed by a tether of translucent tubing, imbedded and taped to her arm.

"Calmly now. It's all right. The hypothermia sent you into cardiac arrest, but you're safe." His smile is bright and wide.

"My voice," she rasps.

"We had to intubate you." At her blank look, he explains, "We had to insert an endotracheal tube to keep your airways clear. The soreness will pass in a few days."

"We?" she whispers.

"Ben and I worked on you together. I'm Shay Gainsboro."

"A doctor?"

He nods. "We looked for ID, but couldn't find any. What's your name?"

Delia's thoughts are a red needle in a cone of frost, sharp clarity in the fog. "Adela," she lies. "Adela Branta."

"Is there someone you'd like me to contact, Adela?"

"I-I don't know." There is a face rendered in a Monet haze but nothing else.

His brow creases. "Can you remember your address or a phone number? Your parents?"

"No."

"Selective amnesia is not uncommon in cases like yours. Try not to be distressed. Recall usually returns in time."

She is not distressed. Should she be?

"Do you know if you have any allergies? Or are taking any medications?"

Delia recollects white tablets that make her queasy and blue ones that force her to sleep—Celexa and Klonopin. But Adela doesn't need psychotropics; Adela wouldn't be bullied into taking medicines she doesn't want to.

She shakes her head. Even whispering hurts, like the time she had her tonsils out. She remembers that too. They gave her ice cream, vanilla with black specks in it—vanilla beans, they said. But it had disgusted her. She'd flushed the polluted confection down the lavatory.

But then, Adela doesn't like vanilla ice cream. Adela likes chocolate. Or maybe mint chocolate chip.

"Are you hungry?" he asks. "Would you like some broth?"

She nods, suddenly craving. Although not food. She wants heat and color.

He returns with a wooden tray and a pastel blue bowl. The broth is topaz au jus and tastes of salt and savory.

He sits attendance on her, watching her eat and making conversation—one-sided entertainment, her eating, his chit-chat. There's a quality to Shay Gainsboro's eyes; they're a silvery gray, like the sky after it rains.

"Now you're awake and eating on your own, the IV can come out tomorrow. You should know you've been in a coma for a few days."

Delia blinks at the news.

"When I pulled you from the lake, I thought you were dead, but there's always a chance with hypothermia. Ben wanted to chopper you to the hospital, but I had emergency defib equipment here. Once we got you stabilized, it was safer not to move you. Ben airlifted in the supplies I needed, and we set up a little ICU for you."

Delia swallows a final spoonful of broth. "Where am I?" she whispers.

"Not far from where you fell in. I live on the other side of the lake."

Delia remembers the swan's words. Lighthouse and train.

He takes away the tray and bowl, and leaves her alone in the white nest.

HOURS PASS, AND she can't sleep. The tube in her arm itches, and besides, she's been asleep for days.

Delia would have put up with the nuisance and the

discomfort, lying there wide-eyed and wakeful. Adela is less forbearing. She peels away the medical tape, grimacing at the smart, and tugs the catheter from her vein. The pinprick hole seeps blood, but stops when she presses a wad of tissue to it.

Standing, she is Delia again, uncertain as she wavers on her feet. Dizzy and weak, she's also mortified by the hospital gown with the immodest gape in the back. Then again, the good doctor undoubtedly put her in it, so he's seen whatever there was for modesty to protect.

Adela yanks off the ugly gown, leaving it in a puddle at her feet. Briefly, she contemplates the sheet. The notion of playing the heroine, draped dramatically in bed linen, appeals; nevertheless, she is tired of white.

She wanders out, bold in her nakedness.

The hallway is full of shadows. Adela dresses herself in those instead, reveling in the luxury of a black cloak draped over bare limbs.

An edge of light pierces her mantle, seepage from the gap between door and carpet. Drawn to it, Adela pads on bare feet to push it open.

At his desk, Shay Gainsboro is startled by her entrance, the glass of amber fluid half-raised to his lips. A second passes, and his arm remembers what it was about; he downs the liquor. But his eyes on her never flicker.

Empty tumbler set aside, he does nothing, says nothing.

Adela slinks in, no longer weak or dizzy, even when she feels her garment of shadows leaching off.

His bed is wide and lush, the antithesis of her narrow, white one. The comforter is a sleek maroon, the sheets burgundy. Slipping into it is like submerging in a velvety merlot, and as intoxicating.

"I can't sleep," she whispers through her cracked throat.

He stands when she reclines, nestled in yards of wine-dark cloth, and joins her.

He tastes of bourbon and the raw tang of heavy mist lying over still water.

When he would be tender, she bites him, raking her teeth across his shoulder. He swears, and she laughs.

All gentleness gone, he pinions her, taking her roughly. Adela glories in his fury, excited by it. She arches to meet him as he plunges through her. Although her eyes are open, a curtain blinks down, and she is engulfed by darkness.

WHEN DELIA OPENS her eyes, she is in her white nest, blinded by the morning sun. She is ashamed, lying naked between the sheets, and isn't sure why. On her pillow is a long, black feather. She regards it, confused, and runs the airy vane through her fingers.

A knock sounds, and she drags the sheet to her chin, tucking the black feather under her pillow. Dr. Gainsboro enters without her invitation. He hefts a traditional doctor's bag in one hand. Draped over the other is a spill of creamy cloth.

"How're you doing this morning?"

Delia recognizes the jaunty tone, ubiquitous to doctorkind, and is conflicted—both soothed and abraded by it.

He nudges aside the discarded IV lines and perches on her bed. Extracting tools from his bag, he checks her blood pressure and shines a light down her throat. His touch is impersonal, clinical and brisk, but she still shrinks away when he pulls aside the sheet so he may listen to her heart—galloping now. His gaze doesn't linger though, and when he is done, he tugs the sheet back into place.

"Everything seems in order," he says. "Any memories coming back?"

"No." More gone, perhaps.

"Well, no worries. Since we don't know of anyone to keep an eye on you, I'd like to keep you here, that is, unless you'd rather convalesce in hospital?"

Delia shakes her head.

"Throat still hurts? Would you like some anesthetic spray? No?"

She's anxious about her voice, knows the risk is greater that she will damage it if she can't feel chafed nerves.

"I brought you a dress. It belonged to my ex, I'm afraid. I hope you don't mind."

Delia shrugs.

"I'm making omelets. Would you like breakfast in bed, or do you feel strong enough to get up?"

There is a sardonic note to his voice that she doesn't understand. "I can come down," she whispers.

He departs to whisk eggs.

The dress is pretty, soft against her skin, with swirling skirts and flowing sleeves. The aroma of fresh coffee and warm bread lures her out.

In a high-ceilinged room with French doors that overlook the lake, a baby grand piano basks in a beam of sunlight. Forgetting her hunger, Delia drifts to the inviting bench and lifts the keyboard cover. She remembers this: satin-finished keys beneath her fingers, the surge of notes in her head.

She plays.

"Ravel isn't it?" Dr. Gainsboro leans against the entranceway wearing a novelty apron patterned like a lab coat.

Delia snatches her hands back, face aflame.

"Please don't stop."

To her chagrin, he parks himself beside her. He splays his fingers on the keyboard and echoes her truncated "*Pavane de la Belle au Bois Dormant*"—except the duet arrangement. She knows this version as well as the solo. Her hands steal to the keys. Delia can no more refrain from playing the counterpart than she can stop her own blood.

The piece is short, only twenty measures.

He begins "*Petit Poucet*," the next composition in the suite, and she is compelled to join in. Halfway through, he disconcerts her by jumping to his feet.

"Crap, the rolls!" He's off and running as she stares.

Belatedly, she smells burning. A miniature breaker of discolored air billows in from the kitchen. The smoke alarm shrills, tardy and unhelpful.

Hands over her ears, Delia hurries toward the commotion, although it feels unnatural to do so. In a room of stainless steel and gleaming ceramic, Dr. Gainsboro utters a stream of profanity as blue as the air, coughing between breaths. The oven fan whirrs, adding its din to the noise pollution—ineffectual despite its racket. A Pyrex baking pan tilts precariously into the sink, its contents exuding a column of smoke, while the doctor waves a towel to dissipate it. It is a futile crusade.

Delia wants to cower, bolt, and burst into tears, but Adela will not let her. As though prescient, she knows to rummage in the adjoining pantry for the broom. It is a high-end model, heavy, with a rubber handle and an attached dustpan. Adela eschews the comfort grip and chokes low, whacking the smoke alarm. Her swing produces a gratifying crunch, and the alarm tips from its spot on the ceiling, dangling from a solitary yellow wire. More importantly, it shuts up.

As she deals with the vexing alarm, Dr. Gainsboro has gained ground on his own campaign. He has flung open the window over the sink and started the ceiling fan, adding its whirling blades to his smoke-dispersing arsenal.

Holding her breath, Adela dashes to the sink and turns on the faucet, dousing the still-smoldering buns.

With the bread extinguished, the crisis is over, and Delia resurfaces. She giggles and regrets it. Smoke scours her lungs, and she doubles over, wracked by coughs.

Dr. Gainsboro swears. He half-carries her through the piano room, the French doors, and onto a wooden deck. He abandons her to gasp on a deck chair while he darts back in. He returns with a glass of water and an olive cylinder, an oxygen tank.

Delia accepts the water, but when he begins tweaking metal knobs, she stays him.

"I'm fine," she rasps.

"You aspirated a lungful of lake water and now smoke," he protests.

Where Delia might have capitulated, Adela is adamant. She shakes her head, and when the doctor seems determined to ignore her, she surges to her feet.

"I said I'm fine!"

Delia is aghast at her outburst, and immediately bereft. Adela has abandoned her. But at least Dr. Gainsboro has stopped unraveling plastic tubing.

She quails and turns her back on his scrutiny. The lake view is breathtaking. Sunlight skims the water, dancing a fairy ballet on the wave tips.

"I'm sorry," she says. "But I can't bear being all wound up in those. Please don't make me."

Delia shivers, feeling winter's nip for the first time. Behind her, Dr. Gainsboro approaches and begins rubbing her arms. His touch is electric and unnerving.

"I'm losing physician points left and right," he says. "Smoke inhalation and now making you stand out here in the cold."

"I'll probably catch pneumonia and die," she says. "And all the other doctors won't let you join in their reindeer games."

He chuckles. "Reindeer games aren't what they're made out to be. Why don't we go inside? I think the place might be aired by now."

She turns, and he is closer than she expected, close enough to make out the individual hairs of his 5 o'clock shadow. Delia blushes and backs away.

His expression flashes from cool disbelief to tender warmth in the span of a blink. She sidles past, face burning.

Within, there is a residual aroma of carbonized dough, but it is tolerable. He goes to close the doors and windows (it puts walls around you), and she creeps straight through into the kitchen and begins scraping the soggy lumps of burned bread down the disposal.

"You don't have to do that."

Delia flinches and hopes he didn't notice. "I don't mind. I can finish making breakfast, if you like."

"That has to be the nicest way someone's told me they're afraid my cooking will burn the house down."

She offers him a shy smile. "Do people tell you that often?"

He winks. "Oh, all the time."

He retrieves a package of Danish from the refrigerator while she tips the well-scrambled eggs into a skillet. They partner well in the kitchen; anticipating her, he hands her spatula and plates, and she is likewise attuned to him, thoughtfully clearing off counter space so he may apportion the pastry.

The breakfast table is a harmonious tableau. Their conversation is undemanding—the weather, the food, the lake. He watches her eat, but his gaze doesn't discomfit her, rather she is flattered. Even when he gives her a pair of yellow pills, she is only curious.

"Antibiotics," he explains. "I'd like you to take them for seven more days."

Obedient, she swallows them. As reward, he clears the table and loads the dishwasher.

While he works, she strays to the piano, drawn to the promise of song held inside the burnished wooden frame. To the accompanying clatter of flatware in the background, she plays. Not Ravel this time, but Tchaikovsky, a composition of water and sky.

In thrall to the piano, she doesn't hear when he comes in, becomes aware of his warmth at her back only during the coda.

"As much as I love having my own personal concert pianist," he says, "you mustn't wear yourself out."

She could play forever; the music flows through her, effortless as sunlight through glass. But she folds her hands in her lap like a good girl and rises from the bench.

"Do you play professionally?" he asks.

She ponders the question as she curls onto the sofa. Adela's voice clamors a warning.

"No," she lies.

"You could." He reclines beside her. She turns bashful and self-conscious; she doesn't know where to look.

"I think we should talk," he says. "I guess this is my cue to apologize about last night, but I honestly can't say I regret what happened."

She is perplexed. "Last night?"

"I've just come out of a bad breakup, and when you came in, I'd already polished off most of that bourbon bottle. It was irresponsible of me, and I wasn't thinking clearly."

Delia doesn't understand what he's saying.

"I want to assure you that I'm not in the habit of sleeping with my patients. Granted, these circumstances are a bit different from my usual doctor-patient associations. Regardless, it was unprincipled."

Buzzing fills Delia's ears, so loud she can't hear him.

"This part I probably shouldn't say, but I'm going to anyway. I'm very attracted to you. After you've fully recovered, I hope, that is, I would like to have a chance to get to know you better on a personal level. But while you're a patient under my care, it would be unethical to resume what we began last night."

The buzzing becomes a hurtful drumbeat in Delia's skull, a pain so intense it paralyzes. She cannot mouth the question she wants to. What is he talking about?

A chime peals through the house.

Begging her pardon, Dr. Gainsboro exits, and voices emerge from the other room: his and another's.

Panic is a wash of ice in her veins, but still she cannot move. Dr. Gainsboro returns. At his side is a strange man, fair where the doctor is dark. The newcomer has tawny hair like unspun flax, and his lanky body vibrates with glad exuberance.

"Adela, this is Ben Rothbart. I'd forgotten he was coming by today. Ben, this is Adela Branta."

Ben extends his hand to her. "At last, the mystery woman has a name."

The obligations of etiquette loosen the paralysis. Delia stands, letting Ben pump her hand, although she finds his vigor draining.

"I hear I owe you thanks for saving my life," she says.

Ben grins. "Nah, it was all Shay here." He delivers a hearty thump to the other man's back. "He's the miracle worker. I've said before the guy could do a triple bypass with nothing but a Swiss army knife and a couple popsicle sticks. All I did was assist and chopper in the popsicle sticks."

She returns his smile, although hers is wan. "Well, this ex-popsicle appreciates it."

The room becomes a jitter of monocular flatness. Delia sways. The morning's events and her off-on-off migraine have frazzled her, and she is abruptly exhausted.

Dr. Gainsboro lays a steadying hand on her shoulder. “Whoops. What did I tell you about taking it easy? It’s officially naptime for you. Let’s get you back to bed.”

He leads her to her room and tucks her in. She is asleep before he leaves.

DELIA’S DREAMSCAPE IS a collage of movement and color. She waltzes in a ballroom, the belle of the party. But her dress bleeds, drenched in a patina of viscous red. A disembodied voice shouts at her missteps. Cigarette smoke mingles with the flailing whiplash of plastic hoses attached to an apparatus of clamps and nozzles.

The dance becomes a tortured reel. She is a marionette. The puppeteer stretches her over a piano soundboard and pounds out a melody. Each note batters, forcing its way into her body until she is torn by the forte piston of hammer on wire. But the wounds are inside, where they don’t show.

Delia jerks awake.

In the dim light of pre-dawn through wooden blinds, she takes in the alien but familiar backdrop of a sumptuous bedroom.

Beside her, Dr. Gainsboro stirs. The press of his nakedness against her own—skin, breath, and cozy warmth—terrify. Last night is a hole in her head.

He reaches for her, strokes a languid hand from hip to breast. “Good morning.” His words are an intimate whisper in her ear. “Remind me never to argue semantics with you. I doubt your definition of ‘fully recovered’ would stand up to a medical textbook’s, but you’ve thoroughly convinced me. I just hope we didn’t wake Ben last night.” He chuckles, soft and low. "Screw that. I hope we did. Serves him right for all those times he kicked me out of the dorm when he had a date over." His hand glides to her thigh. "What say we give it the old college try and make sure he doesn't sleep in?"

"No!" Delia struggles to escape and stifles a cry of relief when he releases her. "I-I should go."

Dr. Gainsboro sighs. "I suppose you're right. I do have to work with the bastard."

She flees. When she achieves the false security of her white nest, she crumples. Her tears saturate the pillow, but although sobs wrack her with the force of machine gun strafe, she makes no sound. She cannot remember why, but it is a rule. If she cries, it must be silent.

When she is empty of tears, Delia wraps a sheet around her shoulders and locks herself in the cool elegance of the guest bathroom. As the shower spits a waterfall of steam, she confronts the red-eyed woman in the mirror.

"You're going insane," her reflection informs her. "Stark raving batty. And also, you've got feathers."

Bewildered, Delia combs several black feathers from her hair. They aren't as long as the one she found yesterday, but there are more. She counts five and pulls a final quill free. Six. Peering close, she probes the line of her part. At her scalp, a row of black pinfeathers protrudes from delicate sheaths.

Nonplussed, she retreats from the mirror.

In the shower, curls of pubic hair swirl down the drain, leaving behind fluffy black down between her legs. The soap catches on the underside of her arms, and her fingertips discover the bristling points of feather follicles pushing through.

She knows these developments should alarm her, but instead she is eased. Feathers are the finest insulation.

There is a white, terrycloth robe hanging on the door, a man's. On her, its hem brushes the ground, and she must roll up the sleeves to find her hands. Still, it is better than a sheet.

Emerging from the bathroom, she hears voices in heated discussion.

"You fucked her?" Ben, astonished and indignant. "What about Lydia?"

"Of the three of us—you, me, and your sister—you're the only one still chasing that dream. Lydia and me, we're through."

"But you don't know anything about this woman. Sure she's hot, but who is she? Don't you find this amnesia line awfully convenient? Damsel in distress with no one to turn to, nowhere to go? It's got scam-the-millionaire stamped all over it."

Delia is sure the thud of her heart will give her away.

"Of course." Dr. Gainsboro's voice is mocking. "How could I not see it? The drowning and hypothermia, the cardiac arrest, she was after my money all along."

"Okay, I'll give you far-fetched there, but just think about what you're doing. Doctors do not sleep with patients. You know the ethics committee would go ape shit. They'd revoke your medical license faster than you could say 'media feeding frenzy.' She could sue you, or worse, blackmail you."

"It's not like that. Ben, I think Adela's the one. My feelings for her are more intense than anything I ever felt for Lydia while we were dating."

"You've known this woman for less than a week. And she was in a coma for most of it!"

"I know. But there's a genuine innocence about her that's just so poignant and so...so *real*. She has this sort of fragile, graceful way of moving that knocks me loopy. When I'm around her, all I want to do is protect her. At the same time, I'm going nuts if I can't touch her. And in bed, my God, the things she can do. She—"

"Okay, whoa! That's enough, big fellah. You're bragging now."

Laughter. "Maybe a little. But you have to understand, there's not a duplicitous bone in her body. Give her a chance and you'll see."

Delia tiptoes back to her room, her head filled with droning confusion. She sits on the bed, lost in oversized folds of terrycloth.

Shay loves me! It is an exultation, but not hers.

Delia huddles in a ball.

What now? Adela is impatient. Didn't you hear? He wants to protect us. He loves us, he loves us, he loves us! And what a ride that boy is too—the feel of him between our thighs, and the way his back bows during orgasm, so totally sexy. Adela rattles on, replaying the sensual details of her trysts with Dr. Gainsboro.

Delia plasters her hands over her ears, but she can't block out Adela's voice. "Stop it," she pleads. "That's dirty talk. We mustn't."

Adela takes pity on her. "Fine, be that way. But don't you like him too? He's nice. And he plays the piano."

Delia uncovers her ears. It's true; he is kind. And he has elegant hands. But what about the other thing, the nightmares and the hurts? What about the bad thing?

Adela is silent. She doesn't have all the answers either.

A polite rapping brings Delia's head whipping up. "Yes?"

The door creaks open. Dr. Gainsboro peeks in. "Are you coming out or would you like to stay in bed today?" There is a glitter in his eyes that makes Delia wish Adela were there. "Ben's putting together breakfast, making sure I don't set the house on fire."

"I don't have anything to wear," she murmurs. "I borrowed your robe."

"And adorable you look in it, too. But I agree we need to get you some clothing, which brings up the rest of the day. Ben's informed me that one of my patients is being troublesome. I've got to chopper into town to check on her. While I'm there, I thought I'd pick up some clothes for you, if you trust my taste. Is there anything in particular you'd like me to get?"

"You're leaving me alone?" Delia is dismayed. "Can't I come with you?"

"You're still recuperating, sweetness—despite your persuasive nighttime arguments to the contrary. It's a fair drive to the heliport, and the chopper ride isn't exactly a walk in the park. Besides, I'm going to be in surgery most of the day."

"Oh."

Dr. Gainsboro crosses the room. Kneeling, he frames her face in his hands and delivers a gentle, chaste kiss on her mouth. "Don't worry, you won't be alone. Ben's going to keep you company while I'm gone. Me and him go way back, and he's a very capable physician. He'll take good care of you. I made him promise not to bite."

He is so earnest; it is contagious and irresistible. She returns his smile.

"That's my girl."

"I-I'll miss you."

His storm-gray eyes soften.

Adela surfaces, crowing. *He's putty, babe. Keep it up.* Delia shoves her aside, and she re-submerges.

"Adela, I know we've just met, and everything about our relationship is irregular. But I'd like you to have something." He fumbles in his pocket and produces a velvet box. Within is a circle of antique filigree, white gold topped by a fiery jewel.

Delia stares.

"It's my great-grandmother's cocktail ring. My mother gave it to me to give to the woman I intended to marry. I would be in heaven if you agreed to be my wife, but you don't have to give me an answer now. I know this is sudden. But yes or no, I want you to have it."

It is Adela who reaches for the ring, puts it on.

Panic-stricken, Delia flies at her, forcing her to retreat. Even so, the ring stays on.

"It's beautiful," Delia murmurs. "But you barely know me. *I* barely know me. What if I turn out to be someone different from who you think I am?"

"Impossible. You're Adela, and I love you."

"The pancakes are getting cold!" Ben's voice interrupts them, breaking into the troubling progression of Delia's thoughts.

Dr. Gainsboro offers her his hand, and she accompanies him to the kitchen.

Ben is surrounded by mounds of flapjacks. More sizzle on the grill beside a pitcher of warming syrup.

In a flawless choreography, he flips pancakes, fetches a trio of mugs from a cupboard, and pours coffee from a burbling pot. It is obvious that he is well acquainted with this kitchen's layout.

"Christ, how many starving African nations did you invite for breakfast?" Dr. Gainsboro joins the dance, depositing plates on the table and pouring milk into a porcelain creamer. They move in practiced synchrony.

Delia is afraid to intrude, and she feels left out, standing in the corridor.

It is Ben who appears at her side and escorts her to her chair. "Poor Adela's been on an IV drip and then subjected to the hazards of your cooking. I figured she's probably ready to gnaw her own arm off."

He drops a napkin in her lap and is away before she remembers to thank him. In short order, he deposits a tower of pancakes on her plate, a mug of coffee, and a glass of juice. Dr. Gainsboro sets out the now-warm syrup.

"Can I help?" she asks.

"Nah. We've got everything covered. Why don't you go ahead and eat before your food gets cold?"

Delia doesn't want to; she was taught that it's bad manners not to wait until everyone is served. But she also doesn't know what to do with her hands or where to look. It unsettles her, seeing these two men working so diligently to serve her.

Adela, exasperated, rescues her. She stirs sugar and milk into her coffee, pours a runnel of syrup, and applies fork and knife to the topmost layer of pancakes. They are luscious—fluffy rapture dissolving on her tongue like maple-flavored snowflakes. She discovers she is ravenous and tucks in.

The men join her only after she has devoured her sizeable portion. The attentive co-host, Ben plunks another stack on the remains of her first.

"See? You *were* starving her," he says.

"Not true!" Adela protests around a mouthful. "It's these pancakes; they're amazing, best I've ever had. They should be illegal."

The men laugh, and all is restful, the quiet punctuated by the clink of silverware and the sounds of chewing. Delia treasures this moment, blankets herself in an aura of well-being and comfort. It is a sort of release, the absence of fear. She knows it is fleeting, but for now, she is at peace.

The swan's words come to her: *peace of heart or a piece of heart.* And her appetite is gone, switched off. She swallows the bite in her mouth and washes it down with juice. It tastes of ashes and brine.

Dr. Gainsboro finishes too and rises. "If I don't skedaddle, the control tower will give me hell."

"A likely excuse," Ben says. "You just want to saddle me with the dishes. Again."

"I'll do them," Delia offers. "It's only fair. You cooked."

Dr. Gainsboro frowns. "No way, missy. I want you to take it easy. Ben's job while I'm gone is to wait on you hand and foot."

"But—"

"Doctor's orders."

"Give it up, honey," Ben laughs. "He's got his stern doctor face on."

Leaving Ben to his good-natured grousing, Delia trails after Dr. Gainsboro as he collects wallet, keys, and little black bag. At the door, he kisses her goodbye. It is neither chaste nor gentle, and Delia is flustered. But Adela isn't. She wraps her arms around his neck and matches his ardor with enthusiasm.

At last, breath ragged and face flushed, he pulls away. "Another one of those and Mrs. Lahey and her angioplasty can go hang."

Happy to oblige, Adela offers herself to him. But he sets her aside, albeit with reluctance, and drives off. As she gazes after his dwindling taillights, Ben enters, drying his hands on a towel.

"It's always the same," he says. "He gets the girl, and I get the dishes."

Delia's face burns. "I really would have been happy to do them."

"And risk the wrath of Shay? Nah. Hey, you know I'm only kidding, right? I don't really mind."

The piano beckons, and Delia gives in. Perching on the bench, she wrestles the robe's overlong sleeves to her elbows.

Ben's eyes narrow and fix on the ornate curlicue of white gold adorning her finger. He frowns at the blood-red facets.

Delia buries her hands in terrycloth pockets, but it's too late.

"You're wearing Shay's family ring," he says.

"He gave it to me," she mumbles, guilty as a child with illicit sweets.

Ben looms close. "You should know something. Shay's like a brother to me." The cheery banter from breakfast is gone. "He's pulled me through some rough times, and I won't let anyone hurt him."

Does he mean *her*? Adela is indignant.

"He's a rich man," Ben continues. "There've been girls in the past who've wanted to take advantage of his generosity and part him from chunks of it. He's been nicer about it than I would've been."

"What would you have done?" Adela asks, seething.

"Kicked them to the curb and sent a pack of snarling lawyers after them."

She lifts her eyes to meet Ben's glower head-on. "Good. Shay's too decent for the likes of gold digging sluts. I'm glad he has a friend like you to watch out for his best interests."

Ben is taken aback by her vehemence and her reply. "Shay's happiness means a lot to me."

"It means a lot to me, too."

He studies her, intent and searching. "I get that."

Adela is mollified, but a simmering undercurrent remains. Delia, diplomat and mediator, nudges her aside.

"Do you play the piano?" She frees her hands. (They have nothing to hide, Adela declares.)

"Not a note. I love music, though; my CD collection could fill this room. Shay tells me you're quite the accomplished pianist."

She lowers her eyes. "He did?"

"Will you play something for me?"

For a change, Delia doesn't need to be coaxed. What should she play? Something clever and quick. Her fingers touch the keys, and the opening measures of Bach's "Invention 4 in D minor" ripple out. It is a good choice. She enjoys the articulate fingering and the playful chase of notes. But it is too short, over too fast, and "Prelude and Fugue in C minor" is underway before she realizes she has decided to keep playing.

She loves how the Prelude begins so somber and then brightens as it approaches the higher registers, and how the solemn Fugue builds to a busy brilliance, driving to a glorious finish. The music swells in her, a twinge that becomes an ache. It wants out, a caged bird beating its wings against the bars of her body.

She hasn't the will to deny it.

When the Fugue ends, she segues to "*Ave Maria*" and unlocks the cage.

Released, the bird takes wing, lifting from her throat in a crystalline soprano. Her voice has recovered from its plunge in the lake and the doctor's endotracheal tube. It soars in a swirl of foreign syllables, reverent and haunting, buoying her with it.

"*Ave Maria, erhöre einer jungfrau flehen.*" The words are meaningless, musical contours and nothing more.

Adela knows what they mean. *Hail Mary, heed a maiden's prayer.* She murmurs a bleak undercurrent beneath Delia's euphoria. *Thou canst hear through the wilderness; thou canst save amid despair.*

Adela's recitation produces a flashbulb pop of memories: an afternoon in a cramped room, foam shells plastering the walls. Delia sings, but takes no joy in it. She is tired, exhausted, but the presence in the other room won't let her stop. Do it again. Get it right.

Safe may we sleep beneath thy care.

She's frightened, always. She thought when the money came, it would be better. But it's not. He is suspicious. He won't let them take her picture, hides her away from the cameras, makes her wear veils and masks.

Though banish'd, outcast, and reviled, O Virgin, see a maiden's sorrow; O Mother, hear a suppliant child.

He comes to her at night. His face is no longer obscured by an Impressionist study of reflected light, the puppeteer from her nightmares, cigarette smoke and shame. Adela protects her, but when he's done, they both weep noiseless tears.

Ave Maria, undefiled, hear a maiden's prayer, and for a father, hear a child.

She remembers what she did, the bad thing that drove her to a freezing lake on a winter night. The pain is punishing, blinding. She slumps over the keyboard, clutching her head. There's a knife behind her eyes, twisting in the gray matter, a hot poker, a zinc-white spike.

"Adela! Christ, what is it?"

She has all but forgotten the man at her shoulder. When he reaches for her, she cries out, writhing away from the solicitous touch. She tumbles off the bench, landing hard. Ben bends to help, and she shrieks. He is too like the other man standing over her. She scuttles back until she is pressed into a corner.

Ben speaks, but his words slur into a senseless gabble juxtaposed with the voice from her dreams. He fumbles with something that glitters like an icicle in the sun and edges closer.

Delia and Adela are bottlenecked. Delia would beg him to leave her alone, give her a moment to repair her tattered sanity; and Adela would tell him to back off, he's freaking her out. But the only thing that comes out is a babble of pleading no's.

The icicle plunges down through terrycloth folds and pierces her thigh. Ben drives the plunger down, filling her veins with ice.

She whimpers and sinks into darkness.

DELIA REMAINS LOCKED in a soporific void, but Adela is awake. The shadows are long, shading her white nest a murky purple. She hears a voice, Ben's, and rises, drawn mothlike to investigate.

Concealed by night's advance, she eavesdrops outside the door.

"—stable and still be asleep when you get here. I stuck her with enough midazolam to keep her out until tomorrow...shit, you think I wanted to? I thought she was going to seize...no, listen to me, she's stable for now so don't wrap your car around a tree. But she's not who you think she is. I heard her sing. She's Delia Cygnet. *The* Delia Cygnet...fuck, would it kill you to turn on a television? She's only the most famous diva in the world, what with everyone baying to get a look at her and now this hubbub. Shay, this is major. They've got an all points on her, think O.J. except substitute her dad for Nicole Brown—"

Adela wields the high-end broom like a cudgel. Retrieved from its new location—propped beneath the broken smoke alarm—it is a familiar weight in her hands. Ben's skull crunches like the defunct alarm, and he topples. Adela clubs him again, just to be sure. Last time, she'd smashed the champagne bottle into Daddy's face until it was a staved-in pulp. But Ben's not family.

She retrieves the cell phone from where it dropped out of limp fingers and clacks it shut. The tinny squawks on the other end cut off.

Adela pauses at the piano, gently pulling the cover over gleaming keys.

Delia slips off the ruby ring and sets it on the mute instrument. Through the French doors, the full moon floats in a blue-black sky, a gleaming beacon warning travelers to beware.

The wooden dock is a slab of ice beneath her bare

feet, but she doesn't feel it. When there are no more planks to cross, Delia unknots the terrycloth sash and lets the robe spill away.

"Adela! Don't!" The anguished shout echoes across the water.

He has flouted stop lights, speed limits, and common sense to get here. Shay Gainsboro sprints to stop her, to save her, but he is too late.

Delia flings herself from the platform. She hangs in the air for a heartbeat, silhouetted by a nimbus of moonlight.

Then she opens her wings.

With a powerful stroke of black pinions, she rises aloft. A white swan swoops to meet her, matching her beat for beat, and the two swans—one black, one white—soar across the lake.

They look back once, in unison, at the dwindling figure on the dock. The man falls to his knees, his face lifted. His features twist as he calls to them.

They vanish into the night sky.

A melody drifts to the grieving man, a duet. Delia and Adela's song is a threnody of heartbreak, despair, and sorrow, and then it too is gone.

"Black Swan, White Swan" is a tribute to one of my favorite ballets, Swan Lake. I'm gaga for its duality and dichotomy: graceful and tragic swan maidens; starkly contrasting black and white costumes; the sensuality and

innocence of Odile/Odette; and the drama and romance of Tchaikovsky's famous score. Acknowledgements and accolades go to Ravel, Bach, Schubert, and, of course, Tchaikovsky for providing me with a soundtrack.

THE BUNNY OF VENGEANCE AND THE BEAR OF DEATH

RABBIT CROUCHED IN a corner, unseen, as the men in the orange jumpsuits slammed their fists into the bad man. She preened her ears as a heavy foot dislocated the bad man's kneecap and twitched her whiskers when the bad man screamed in pain. His shrieks seemed to encourage the other men to greater excesses of violence. Blood splattered the dingy white walls.

Rabbit's eyes gleamed gold, and her nose wiggled at the tang of copper in the air.

"Bunny?" A great round paw, shaggy of fur and sharp of claw, appeared through the solid wall. A second joined it, and then the jagged muzzle, thick shoulders, and burly haunches of Bear entered the cell. The men continued their sport.

Rabbit raised a paw and sketched in the air. She left behind sparkling trails of words in an archaic script older than memory. Bear could read them for he, like Rabbit, remembered a time when the stars moved in a different dance and the mountains were young.

Yes, O Bear of Reason? Rabbit wrote. The words hung like gossamer threads before fading away.

"What're you doing?" Bear said.

Rabbit's paws flowed through the air in a ballet of lettering, leaving behind spangled words in her wake. *I am overseeing my domain, O Bear. That man yonder*, and she dipped her nose at the flailing, screaming bad man, *abducted three young boys and took his pleasure of them, reveling in his own brutality. Thereupon he strangled them, tore out their eyes, and cut off their youthful manhoods as trophies.* She stroked a paw over her soft ear. *He also drowned five kittens and crucified a puppy.*

Bear read her words with great solemnity. He nodded his head as she listed the man's crimes. "But what are *you* doing here, Bunny?"

I am fulfilling my purpose. I heard the prayers of the kittens as death water closed over their heads, and I felt the rage in the heart of the second boy's father when he saw the mutilated remains of the joy of his soul.

"I thought we agreed not to get involved anymore."

O Bear of Reason, you and our celestial brethren decided to withhold your influences. If you will search your memory, you will remember I kept my own counsel.

Bear sat on his haunches. "That's not nice, Bunny. I should take you back to the sky pagoda."

Rabbit lifted a hind leg and scratched at a spot behind her ear. "Don't be such a pook head." Her voice was high and nasal. It squeaked out of her throat as though squeezed from a crowded chamber.

She raised her paw and continued writing. *The object of my attentions will soon flow from my jurisdiction to yours, if you wish to take him.*

Bear glanced at the bloody figure in the corner. The bad man had lost consciousness. A thickset man with a tattoo of a red scorpion on his arm lifted him up.

"You won't hop away, will you?"

I will stay, she sketched in the air.

Bear lumbered forward as the scorpion-tattooed man bashed the bad man's skull against the steel lavatory. He reached into the broken man's chest with a sharp-clawed paw. He groped for a moment and then pulled forth a murky shape that jiggled in his grasp. Bear sat down, lifted his paw to his mouth, and popped in the oozing grayness. In a single gulp, it was gone.

Blood and brain matter spilled from the dead man's cracked skull.

"See?" Rabbit said. "Wasn't that yummy?"

"I suppose." Bear licked his muzzle. "Will you come with me to the sky now, Bunny?"

I do not wish to return, O Bear of Death. You are stronger than me, and larger, so you may force me if you will. She thumped her foot on the smooth cement. "But you won't, will you?"

"Why don't you want to come back?"

A ribbon of elegant script streamed from Rabbit's paw. *When I saw that words would not sway our kindred nor the fire of vengeance kindle them, I kept myself quiet and still. You may do as you like, O Bear of Reason, but I will perform my function.*

Suddenly, Rabbit's ears pricked up. She snuffled the air, her pink nose busy. "Hsst! I smell a bad man." Her paw flashed. *I hear the thoughts of a murderer, unrepentant. He raped five women and forced them to swallow a poison that burned through their bodies. They died screaming in agony, vomiting up their innards.*

She leaped into the air, but Bear reached out. He caught one of her strong hind legs and shook her by it. "Bunny, no. I invoke your other manifestation. No longer Bunny of Vengeance, I appeal to Bunny of Words."

Rabbit hung upside down from Bear's paw; her long ears trembled. "I wanna smack the bad man."

"This place is full of bad men. They are being punished for their crimes without your intercession. Justice has been done."

"Justice isn't vengeance and you know it." Rabbit swung in Bear's grip as she sculpted the air. *And you know as well as I that justice is neither swift nor true in the world of man.*

Bear tipped his head so he could better read Rabbit's inverted script. "I know. But it's no longer your job to watch over them."

"Is so."

"Is not." Bear turned, still dangling Rabbit by her hind leg, and jumped.

Both animals passed cleanly through the stone and metal walls, and fell through the open air outside. They plummeted several stories before landing softly, cushioned by Bear's wide paws. Bear padded past the guard towers and razor wire. Large searchlights swept over them. They elicited no outcry.

"You're not taking me back," Rabbit said. "If you do, I won't talk to you ever, ever again."

Bear found it awkward walking on only three legs. "You don't mean that."

"Well, maybe for a week. And anyway, I'll wait until you fall asleep, and I'll hop away. You can't stop me, and you know it."

Bear broke into a clumsy trot as they cleared the penitentiary gates. The scenery around them flickered by in a blur of shadow and light. "I'm not taking you back. We're going to a special place, one dedicated to both of us."

"Vengeance and death? Really?" Rabbit clapped her paws together. "Yay!"

"Not those, the other ones. Reason and words."

Bear halted. Rabbit twisted her body so she could take in their destination. A plaque at the top of a large set of stairs, watched over by two stone lions, read: *New York Public Library*.

Bear lollopped up the steps. His paws were too large to take them individually, and he stumbled, off-balance.

"You're gonna topple us over," Rabbit said. "Put me down."

"Hush." Bear shifted Rabbit from his paw to his mouth, clamping his teeth over her ears.

"You're getting my fur all goopy."

Bear did not reply, as his mouth was full. He bounded up the stairs and passed through the glass doors, swiveling his head from side to side, searching. Rabbit flopped back and forth in his mouth. He carried her over to a thick, much-handled tome lying open upon a podium and dropped her on the bared pages.

She glanced down. "Webster's? Fooie. I want the Oxford English one."

Bear dropped to his haunches. "Sorry."

Rabbit, her eyes wide and reverent, gazed at the different colored spines, lined up neatly around them. "Lookit all the words." She breathed in, her nose atwitch. "All the words and words and words and words."

Bear put a paw gently on Rabbit's head. "Feel better now?" He watched her swivel around, her eyes bright and glowing at the array of books.

Rabbit rose on her hind legs. *I was fine before, O Bear of Reason*, she wrote. *But I have always found temples of devotion to me and mine soothing.*

"Me too." Bear surveyed the tall shelves lined with scientific journals bound by year and series. "Here in our shared holy place, I think we should talk."

Very well. Let us converse.

"I don't think you should go around revenging people."

"How come?"

"We agreed to leave the world alone."

You may have done so, but I did not concur. I do a service for the wheels of balance. I am karma. I am righteousness. If I do not oversee my domain, then who will punish the wicked?

"You are not improving the balance, Bunny. You're making it worse."

Rabbit stomped her hind leg. "I am *so* doing good!" Her paw darted in the air. *In bygone eras, crimes such as the ones I read in the minds of those men carried true penalties—entrails torn from flesh and salted with brine, skin flayed from bones, the sear of red-hot iron. What is the penalty now? A few years in a clean room with regular meals, and then returned whole and hale so they might wreak havoc anew? Or at best a quick, clean death? Where is the fairness in that? Where is the right?*

"It isn't up to you anymore. The man who killed those children—did it help them, what you made the other men do to him? Did it bring back his victims, erase their suffering?"

Of course not, O Bear of Reason. But he will not commit new atrocities.

"He wouldn't have anyway. He was serving a life sentence."

Rabbit ignored the interruption. *And the kinfolk of the slaughtered will hear of it and rejoice.*

"What of the criminal's loved ones? Won't they be sad?" Bear closed his eyes. "I tasted a sister on that man's soul." He smacked his mouth. "She cherished her brother, sins and all. Won't she grieve?"

Rabbit crossed her paws and glared. "What's your point?"

"You do harm. Leave the world of man to itself. In the end, I will take them all."

"Easy for you to say. Everything comes to you. But so what? Death doesn't solve anything. It just finishes it."

Bear sighed, a great exhalation that fluffed through Rabbit's fur. "Death solves everything, O Rabbit of Words and Vengeance."

"Wanna bet?"

Bear eyed Rabbit. "What sort of bet?"

Rabbit's paw, limned in spangled light, became a blur of motion. *Relinquish the life of the man you took. We will watch him and work upon him together. I will work one instance of my aspect on him. You work one of yours. Then we'll see which way leaves the world the better.*

Bear considered this.

But only our eternal aspects, O Bear of Death. If reasonable words were enough to sway men's hearts, then vengeance would be unnecessary.

"Death versus vengeance? If I win, you come back to the sky pagoda with me. No more Bunny of Vengeance hippity-hopping about."

And if I am victorious, you must accompany me on this plane as I will it, and together, we will cut a swath of retribution and death as this time has never seen before. Agreed?

Bear nodded. "I get to choose what parts we visit, and I get to go first."

So be it.

Bear concentrated. His muzzle twitched and his jaws strained apart. He gave a great cough, spitting up a viscous gray ball. It bumped and rolled to a stop on the thin library carpet.

Rabbit bounded off the podium and landed beside it. She jabbed a paw at the globule and peered in. Close up, the gray resolved into a snarl of many colors, swirled together into a morass of gray. "This one's all messy."

"They usually are."

She pulled her paw out, dragging a colorless line. "I got the beginning."

Bear plucked Rabbit from her perch and wrapped her in a hug. "Best you pull hard."

Rabbit yanked. The lump of life unraveled in a shining filament. It unkinked itself—for a moment, a single strand before them. She gave the end in her paws another tug and it wrapped around and around as they watched. At last, the end knotted itself anew and the man's life sprang up around them.

"IS IT A boy or a girl?"

"A boy, Mrs. Highland. A wonderful, healthy baby. Have you thought of a name?"

"His father's name was Jacob."

Rabbit sat in a corner and eyed the squalling newborn, a shriveled red bundle of flailing limbs.

"You could take him now, at the very beginning. Then he wouldn't live to hurt anyone. You gonna?"

"Nope."

"I didn't think so."

AS HE DID every school morning, Jacob knocked on the door of his sister, Ellie's, room. He juggled a ragged backpack over his arm and a windbreaker a size too small.

He heard a soft moan from within.

Jacob dropped his pack and pushed open the door. Instead of finding Ellie dressed and ready, she lay curled up in bed, huddled under the covers.

He ran to her side. "What's the matter, El?"

"My stomach hurts."

"Your stomach always hurts. You gotta get up." He tugged on the blankets to uncover his sister's slender frame, the nightshirt she wore revealing bruises in various stages of healing covering her legs and arms. He was accustomed to seeing the purple, yellow, and black hurts on his sister's body; they matched his own.

"Stop it, Jakie. I'm really sick."

Jacob shifted from foot to foot. "Can't you be sick at school?"

"Get your asses out here!" Their mother's voice rang through the tiny house. The thin walls bounced the sound in the confined area, warping and magnifying it.

"It hurts," Ellie whispered.

The sound of heavy footsteps brought both pairs of eyes to the door. Sister and brother shared a fearful look.

The door slammed open. Their mother stood in

the entrance, glowering. Her mouth twisted, the red lipstick she wore stark on her pale features.

"What are you doing in here?" Before Jacob could answer, she grabbed a handful of his hair. "You filth!" Pinioning him in place, she punctuated every other word with an echoing slap. "I told you never to go in your sister's room. You're never to touch her, ever, ever, ever."

Rabbit watched as Mama rained blows on the boy. *Do you intend to take the woman?* she wrote. *Perhaps truncate the root cause of the maddening guilt that roils in his mind?*

"Nope."

Rabbit shrugged.

THE RAIN WAS cold, and the eyes of the man in the purple sweater, colder. But the hollowness in Jacob's belly made him reckless. Twenty bucks would buy some food, and maybe the man's place would be warm. Surely, nothing he wanted Jacob to do could be worse than starving.

"Bear?"

"Not now either."

"But if you take that man, it'll stop him from making a bad man out of—"

"No."

ELLIE SMILED, RADIANT in her white, sequined gown, her sandy hair peppered with rice, as she drew her brother into an embrace. "I'm so glad you could make it to the reception."

Her hug was tender. Jacob broke from it. As he always did, he felt like he was sullying Ellie by touching her, being near her. Yet at the same time, he yearned to hold her in his arms, like they used to do when they were children. She was the sanctuary, the harbor he'd always looked to.

And now she belonged to someone else.

The woman's mate would be a beneficial choice, Rabbit wrote. *I can scent the violence and anger fermenting in her groom. For many years he will belittle a psyche already traumatized, and it will place a wedge between brother and sister. Removing him now would revive their relationship, mend it before it becomes forever sundered.* Rabbit let her paw droop to her side. "And the bad man would have Ellie back before she gets all broken and sad—"

"Not him neither."

"When're you going to do it?" Rabbit knew she was whining, but she was growing antsy, seeing all these unpleasant scenes of the bad man's life. It was enough that he had been wicked. She didn't like standing witness to these previous episodes. It did not matter that he too was a victim, that others had helped to spawn the monster he had become.

"I will when I'm ready," Bear said.

THROUGH THE PRICK-PRICK-PRICK in his mind, Jacob could hear the voices, though he struggled to shut them out. He was disgusting, an animal, to even think those thoughts. Touching, skin upon skin, the taste of sweat in his mouth, the living warmth salty against his tongue. It was wrong to yearn for such comforts. Evil.

His mother had known from the beginning about the disease, the sin festering in him. There were pictures of him as a baby, dressed in pretty dresses with yellow bows in his hair. Mama delighted in showing them to him, proving that she had tried so hard to fix him, make him clean and nice, like Ellie.

But if you mixed shit with water, you didn't get half shit and half water, you got shit. That's what Mama always said.

The puppy had been dirty too. He'd licked it clean, but it had still been dirty. There was nothing else he could do. He despaired when he realized it would grow up, awash in sin. The devil was in all beasts.

Until God had told him how to save it. He'd shown him through his holy son.

Rabbit lifted her paw. *He has crossed the precipice. Linger, and he will beget only evil. If you took him now, you would prevent the deeds before him from transpiring.*

"I know."

And still you refrain?

Bear met her question with silence.

THE VOICES BATTERED inside his head. Jacob lifted his eyes to the clear partition, the bulletproof glass. No one ever visited him.

The whispers and chants in his skull silenced when he saw the woman watching him, tears bright in her eyes.

"Ellie, what are you doing here?" His voice was dull, although his heart tripped in his chest, so fast, so hard. Had it been beating before?

"Aren't they feeding you in there, Jakie? Why didn't you call me?"

"You know."

"I don't. No matter what they say you did, no matter if you actually did those things. It's not your fault. When Mama—"

"Go ahead and say it."

Her voice faltered. "You're not a bad person. I

know you're not."

"I am. I have been since I was born. Mama knew it from the start. She tried to save me, but I was too evil."

"That's not true!"

"I don't want you coming back here. I don't want you seeing me again."

"Jacob—"

"Go away."

"I'll always love you."

Jacob waited for the voices to shrill their mockery and jibes. Love wasn't for him. He wasn't good enough for it.

They remained uncharacteristically silent.

The guard stepped forward. Their time was up.

"I'll get you out of there," Ellie said. "We need to be there for each other, help each other. Like when we were kids, remember?"

Jacob touched his hand to the thick, smeared glass. "Ellie—"

Here is proof that my services are still required, O Bear of Death, Rabbit sketched in the air. *Through a quirk of man's justice, he will be released. Will you take him before he is freed to wreak more havoc in the wide world?*

Bear shook his head.

THE STREET LIGHT was still out, the sickle moon the only illumination. The city didn't bother fixing it anymore. It had been dark for years. Still, Ellie would call the utility people again. Maybe they'd listen to her this time.

She hated walking home at night, especially having to pass through this one, dark block.

Why have you brought us to this moment, O

Bear? The evil man is not present.

"Watch, Bunny."

In the darkness, Ellie didn't see the cluster of men waiting for her in the shadows.

Rabbit's ears flickered. "You going to take the head bad guy? Ellie might get away if you do."

"No."

The two animals watched as figures coalesced from the gloom, surrounded Ellie, and cut off her retreat. They were featureless in makeshift masks and shrouded by the night.

"Pretty lady, let's have your purse."

Ellie froze. Her handbag was full of the tips her customers had given her that night. She needed that money, and safety was one block away—bright lights and populated streets.

Putting her head down, she charged, knocking into the man in front of her. He went down, oaths spilling from his lips. But the man beside him leaped, tackling her before she could make good her escape.

They didn't like it when their victims fought back. To teach her a lesson, they tore her clothes off, raped her, beat her with bricks and boards, and left her bleeding, broken, and half-dead on the ragged pavement.

Rabbit knew a passerby would find her and summon aid shortly. Ellie would survive. But the bad man would learn of the assault. It would break his mind, shatter him when he learned of her violation. While she lingered in the hospital, mending from her injuries, he would succumb, totally and utterly, to the voices in his mind.

Bear put Rabbit down and padded forward on his wide paws. He reached into Ellie's broken body and drew out, with infinite care, a flickering shape—her soul. He inserted it into his toothy maw and swallowed.

The woman's watery breathing stopped, and a burr hummed from her chest—the rattle of death's embrace. She lay still.

"I am done," Bear said.

"You killed *her*," Rabbit said. Her eyes glistened; she blinked. Tears darkened her fur and trembled on her whiskers. "She was the only good thing in his life. How could you take *her*? How could you?"

Bear picked Rabbit up and rocked her in his paws. "Shh, little bunny. Don't cry. They all die. It is the way of things."

"But she was good!"

"The good die as well as the bad." Bear pushed his paw at the shining image before them. "If you wish it, his purpose can now be for vengeance. In avenging her death, he will act justly."

Bunny rubbed her eyes with a paw. With the other, she shaped words in the air. *What would be the point? It would not fix the wrong.*

"Exactly." Bear took the life string out of Rabbit's paws and flung it away. It shrank, growing dimmer and dimmer until it was a single shining mote of light, then nothing. Gone.

"When bad things happen, it hurts," Rabbit whispered. "It makes me sad and frightened. I want to fix it. Make it better."

"Poor Bunny." Bear cuddled her against his chest. "There is no fairness, no true justice. There is only what we make, here and now—and then there is me. You can't change that, little one. No matter how many bad men you get, there will be other bad men, bad women, and bad things that happen."

Rabbit sobbed. "I don't like it down here anymore! It's scary and mean. I want to go home."

Bear nuzzled her head. "I won't let the bad things hurt you. I'll keep you safe, and I'll take care of you forever and ever."

Rabbit sniffled. "Promise?"

"Promise."

Bear leaped, sending them hurtling into the sky. He carried Rabbit, still weeping softly, in his arms.

As I've mentioned elsewhere, I've come to regard the rabbit as something of a personal totem animal. In addition to its grace and winsome features, and its fanciful personality, it possesses a long and mystical heritage. In our house, bunnies are regarded as fierce, sometimes savage creatures, the kind of animal you'd think of as a mascot for a sports team, alongside tigers and falcons. Makes perfect sense to me…

A NOSE FOR MAGIC

I THOUGHT I was just being a normal guy when the first thing that dazzled me about Lauren was her fragrance. I would discover it was about as normal as metal-noise-grindcore-ambient music. But working in the computer lab that day, I was transfixed by her scent. It was a floral blend—hibiscus, wild tulip, and honeysuckle—nice, but standard. But as she explained how her pet had mauled a semester's worth of research papers, all stored on the CD she brandished, I caught a trace of dark chocolate and balsam, and like a memory of sweetness, honey. The combination was so unusual, I barely heard her. I only realized she'd finished talking when she handed me her disc.

Obvious teeth marks stippled and scraped along it. Cat, perhaps? Or maybe a toy poodle?

"I don't know if I can salvage anything," I said. "In the future, there's this thing you can do to prevent losing data—"

"Make backups?" I scented cayenne pepper and cardamom. It matched her tone, arch and rueful. "I assure you, that lesson has been seared into my psyche."

I grinned. "Maybe we'll get lucky."

Ginger and white pepper.

I spritzed the CD with fix-it solution. I had my doubts, but this stuff was the closest thing to a miracle I had. The acrid smell blotted out her perfume, clearing my sinuses like a sluice of ice water.

When I finished wiping the disc, the scarring was gone. "This doesn't look so bad." I stuck it in my drive.

Vanilla and fig.

Was she carrying a spice rack? My nose is quirky sensitive, which has its drawbacks when I'm in classes filled with techie geeks who can hack any software program but can't figure out the proper application of soap. Now it had me good and truly confounded.

"What perfume are you wearing?" I blurted.

"I'm not. Can't stand the stuff."

"Huh." The drive whirred like a trooper, giving its all. It could've been singing Gilbert and Sullivan for the life of me. "Do you use a special shampoo?"

She tugged at her hair, auburn and wavy. "Nope. Just some drugstore brand; I think it's supposed to smell like blueberries. That affects my CD how?"

"Oh, sorry." My face heated several degrees. "I just wondered."

"That makes two of us."

"Huh?"

She tapped my monitor. "Is it working?"

"Uh. I mean, yeah. I'm reading your files."

"Thank God!" She leaning over the desk and kissed my cheek. "And thank *you*."

I lost sensation in my toes and fingers as all the

blood vacated my extremities. "N-no problem. Want me to burn you a backup?"

"A thousand yeses."

I fumbled a blank disc out and stuck it in the burn tray. While the computer hummed to itself, a heady bouquet of wild sage and red wine permeated the air.

"You've just saved two lives, y'know," she said. "I was ready to skin Koushee and then throw myself off the roof of the astronomy building."

Circulation dribbled back to my brain piecemeal. "Koushee's your cat?"

"Skunk, actually."

"You have a *pet skunk*?"

She laughed. "Sometimes animals choose you instead of the other way around. Don't worry, he's de-scented."

The computer flashed triumphantly.

I ejected both discs. "My name's Derek, in case you have any more skunk-damaged CDs."

"I'm Lauren. And I won't, or if I do, I'll be too busy having an aneurism to make it to the lab."

"In that case, my shift ends in ten minutes. You want to get some coffee or something?" I couldn't believe how cool that'd come out. Usually, with members of the XX set, I hem and stutter, an unfortunate shortcoming that becomes pathetic and tragic the prettier they are. And Lauren was a hottie by anyone's standards.

"Sure," she said, "except I'm not a coffee person. Want to meet my skunk and have some tea instead?"

"Yes!" was out before she was done asking.

Lauren lived off campus, a short stroll from the computer lab. When she opened her door, a strange smell wafted through—burnt cinnamon or allspice. It wasn't unpleasant, certainly better than eau de overflowing cat box, the prevailing aroma in my ex-girlfriend's place.

I trailed along, sniffing. "Is that incense?" I asked.

In her cramped kitchen, Lauren set a dinged kettle on the stove. "What is it with you and smells?"

Before I could answer, a pair of glowing green orbs peeped around the corner.

"Cripes!"

The green eyes resolved into a pudgy animal. It was tawny buff with stumpy legs, a huge bush of a tail, and entirely non-scary brown eyes. It waddled over, and the kitchen's overhead revealed a pair of cream stripes down its back.

"That's Koushee." Lauren swept the animal into her arms. "Say hello to Derek, you brat. He's the reason you're not a stole."

Koushee's wedge-shaped head swiveled to follow me, nose snuffling.

"This is the little guy who chewed up your disc?"

"The stinker snagged it from the coffee table when I wasn't looking. By the time I caught him, he'd gotten a couple good chomps in." She ruffled the fur behind his ears. "Fuzzbutt here likes shiny things."

"I've never seen a skunk this color before." Or this close.

"He's an apricot chip. Most people don't realize they come in more than black and white."

"Can I pet him?"

"Fine by me. He'll let you know if he's not keen about it."

He didn't bite when I reached out, which I took as consent. His fur was lush and silky. Skunks were soft. Who knew?

The kettle gave a plaintive wail from the stove, and Lauren dumped Koushee to the linoleum. She spooned tea leaves from a tin into a cast-iron teapot which bore a striking resemblance to the critter at our feet, having two eyes at the base of the spout and a pair of round ears near the handle. Four stubs at the bottom could've been legs, and an off-center bulge a tail.

"Is that a skunk teapot?"

"Now what sort of whacko would come up with a skunk teapot?" She winked. "It's a tanuki, a Japanese raccoon dog. There's a long history of tanuki tea kettles. They're supposed to be magical."

She held out the tin. "Sniff?"

Pretty girl says sniff, I sniff. I got a noseful of juicy guava, delicate marigold, and violets.

"What is it?"

"A blend I special order. Wait 'til you taste it."

She poured boiling water into the tanuki kettle. I half-expected it to yelp and scamper off, but it sat like a good teakettle while aromatic steam drifted from its spout. If the dry leaves had smelled good, the addition of hot water made them phenomenal. Without asking, Lauren spooned dark honey into my mug. She also filled a shallow saucer with tea, blowing it cool before setting it down.

"For Koushee?"

"If I don't give him any, he sulks."

Leaving the skunk to his tea, we took ours into a crowded living room. Along one wall was a floor-to-ceiling bookshelf filled with tomes in various stages of worn. They were stacked vertically and horizontally, leaning, listing, and separated by the odd knickknack. A plush fox was wedged between a stack of tattered paperbacks, a plastic gargoyle crouched in the arch formed by two hard covers, and a jagged, black rock propped up a tower of mismatched spines.

Lauren lounged on a brown futon couch—the only seating—and I perched beside her to sip my tea. I burned my tongue.

"Good, huh?"

"Mmm." I puffed at the steam whorls, stifling a pained whimper.

"Want a cookie?" From beneath the futon, Lauren retrieved a box featuring a picture of Beatrix Potter's Peter Rabbit. "Amaretto biscotti, actually."

I doubted my scalded tongue was up for biscotti. "That's a strange place to keep food."

"Koushee stuck them there." Lauren bit the ears off a bunny.

"Your skunk seems to get into a lot of stuff." I risked another sip. No burn this time, and yes, it *was* good.

"He's high maintenance, but I like that he's clever. Plus, most witches don't think to cast hexes against skunks."

I remembered to swallow my mouthful of tea. "What?"

"Cats are common; everyone has a cat. Dogs and ferrets too, these days. I'm as surprised as the next gal to have ended up with a skunk as a familiar, but really, skunks are ideal: curious, intelligent, sensitive. He's also a great lap warmer in winter."

The strangest thing was happening. My thoughts kept leapfrogging away from coherent sentences. While Lauren spoke, I submerged deeper and deeper into a boggy, green-tea morass. A stream of headlines about drugged drinks and black market kidney harvesting spooled through my head, but they spooled right out again.

While I blinked in a tea daze, Koushee trundled in.

"Skunks also have impeccable timing." Lauren set aside her mug so she could hoist him into her lap.

She pet him—long, languid strokes. His eyes glowed that disturbing green, but this time it didn't faze me. After all, Lauren's eyes were glowing too.

Although I knew something queer was happening, I sat blissfully frozen, at peace with the world. A quiet grunting, between an oink and a purr, thrummed through the room. Koushee, of course.

Lauren thumped my chest, and her hand sank in wrist-deep. I didn't stir, although a part of me was hollering and having hysterics. It didn't hurt, more like a warm tingle. She yanked, and there was a squirming shape, all claws and teeth, gripped in her fist. The creature (lizard?) spread a pair of fleshy wings (bat?) and sank its fangs (snake?) into her thumb.

Lauren yelped, which shook off some of my paralysis, and flung the thing away. The lizard/bat/snake slithered into her kitchen. Koushee sprang after it.

"Dammit!" She chased after both, and sounds of breaking dishware crashed out.

The hysterical me was building up momentum.

"Derek!"

Still, a pretty girl in distress trumped hysterics.

In the kitchen, Lauren crouched over Koushee. The skunk was backed in a corner, tail fluffed to its full spread. He clamped the lizard-thing's thrashing wing in his jaws and clutched the rest between his front paws.

"No bite! Drop it!"

Koushee hissed.

Lauren held out her hand. "Give it."

The skunk eyed her.

"Give the nasty to Mommy. Do you want a cookie? Nice cookie?"

It seemed Koushee thought the proposed trade equitable; he let Lauren have his prize. She had a Tupperware container in her other hand—a long, skinny one, the right size for uncooked spaghetti. She shoved the lizard-thing in and snapped the lid shut.

"Derek, get me the duct tape. In there, above Foxy."

I charged to the other room. On the shelf over the toy fox, a roll of gray tape had been jammed between a pair of tattered paperbacks. I snagged it, starting a waterfall of books, and dashed back.

Muttering to herself, Lauren unwound a length of tape. Still clutching the spaghetti container, she used a steak knife to cut the strip free. Some of it doubled over, sticking to itself and twisting into a messy ribbon. I steadied the Tupperware for her while she sealed it shut.

Close up, the lizard/bat/snake turned out to be none of the above. Aside from having wings, it scrabbled at the plastic of its prison with six sets of wicked claws on the ends of its six spiny legs—which Biology 101 informed me was scientifically improbable for either mammal or herp.

I felt a nudge at my ankle. Koushee wobbled on his hind legs, his front paws waving in the air.

"Could you get him a treat?" Lauren asked. "Skunk cookies are in the drawer by the sink."

Uncooked spaghetti and shards of porcelain

ground underfoot as I offered Koushee a bone-shaped biscuit from the drawer. He snatched it and trotted into the living room. Lauren tailed him, and I followed her.

The skunk disappeared beneath the futon and crunching sounds ensued.

"So, who did you piss off?" Lauren plopped down.

I sat beside her, mostly because otherwise, my knees would've folded where I stood.

"I saw you'd been marked at the computer lab," she continued, "but didn't realize it was a curse until Koushee told me."

"Koushee *talks to you*?"

She squinted. "You seriously have no clue, do you? Derek, sweetie, I'm a witch. Magic's for real."

"Nuh-uh. I'm a Protestant."

"Oh dear. Okay, look." She hopped up and grabbed the plush fox from the bookshelf. "Here." She plunked it in my lap.

The fox had two shiny, black button eyes, and a fuzzy crimson coat that had seen better days.

"Thanks?" It smelled like my grandmother's attic, lavender and dust.

"*Oracle fox*," Lauren said, "*fox so bright, share your voice, share your sight.*"

"Excuse me?"

She blushed. "I was eight when I wrote that spell. At the time, it seemed like a good idea to imbue Foxy with the oracle voice, and I thought rhyming couplets were the height of sophistication."

The fox wiggled and opened its soft muzzle. "*A curse reveals a nose for magic*," it said.

I almost chucked it across the room, but Lauren leaned to hear the fox-spouted doggerel, giving me a straight-on view of her cleavage.

"*Avert with charm a fate most tragic*," the fox chanted. Its voice was high-pitched and nasal, with a smug, lisping quality. "*Bring the curse to its maker; break the spell to forsake her.*"

I turned the fox upside down, looking for a battery hatch or a pull string, or better yet, an off switch.

"*Avert a witch's hex, don't kill her.*"

It kept talking, even upside down. No off switch either.

"*A life mundane or so familiar.*"

Nope, I couldn't deal. "I need to go." I stood.

"Don't be silly. Sit down and finish your tea."

For a whole half-second I considered going against my hardwired, guy conditioning. But Lauren remained a pretty girl, albeit one with a prophesizing stuffed animal. I sat, lifted the half-empty, lukewarm mug of tea from the futon's arm, and downed it.

Even tepid, the stuff was good. I swallowed, and sunflower petals with a hint of cocoa beans lingered on my tongue. The skip-hop of my heart mellowed, and adrenalin-knotted muscles unkinked.

Lauren set the spaghetti container on the floor and stepped to her bookshelf. As soon as her hand passed over the black stone, I smelled ginseng and menthol.

"What's that rock?"

"Smoky quartz. Why?"

"Did you douse it in some Chinese herbal concoction?"

Her eyes widened. "Is that what you smell?"

"Don't you?"

She glanced at the plush fox. "*A curse reveals a nose for magic.* I was going to ask if you see things other people don't—"

"Nothing comes to mind."

"But now I want to know how long you've been sniffing the unusual."

"Define 'unusual.'"

"Strange, heady scents that other people don't notice."

"That's not magic. That's having a good sense of smell."

"Foxy says no."

"If a stuffed fox says so, it must be true."

Lauren grinned. "I *said* I was eight. C'mon, work with me. When was the last time your nose got overwhelmed by something extraordinary or distinctive?"

"Aside from you?"

"Aside from me."

Megan's cat box came to mind, but it seemed unchivalrous to bring up my ex's housecleaning shortcomings.

Koushee emerged from the recesses of the futon, biscuit crumbs clinging to his whiskers. He stuck his paw on my ankle, and I was immersed in scent memory: rancid fat and decaying flesh steeped in ambergris and ammonia. I gagged. Koushee removed his paw, and the smell was gone.

"What is it?" Lauren asked. "You've turned green."

"Megan's apartment. It was disgusting and...and *wrong.*"

"Who's Megan?"

"My ex. When we started going out she smelled like peaches and cloves."

"And then?"

"Last week, I was staying over at her place, and,

well, 'overwhelmed by something extraordinary or distinctive' sums it up, but not in a good way."

"Did you eat or drink anything there? A curse needs to be imbibed."

"She cooked dinner. Mac and cheese."

Lauren nodded. "Then what?"

"A *stink* woke me in the morning, so bad I almost puked. I thought it was her cat box. I grabbed my pants and bolted. Ended up calling later and breaking it off over the phone. Not my finest hour, but the thought of meeting up with her in person started my eyes watering."

"Yep, Megan cursed you, all right. Don't feel too bad. It's common for noobs to try to explain the magical with the mundane."

"She cursed me because of the break up?"

"Actually, no, she cursed you before that—although dumping someone over the phone is way up there on the curse-worthy front. But it seems you are what we call a *feral.* See, magic is mostly genetic—our crowd is way inbred—but sometimes folks dripping with power pop onto the scene, ones who don't have a sage or seer anywhere in their bloodline. I'm thinking Megan triggered a feral defense mechanism because a magic schnozzle is near unheard of, so she wouldn't have prepped for it. It probably saved you from being thralled to her."

"Thralled? What's *thralled*?"

"Thrall is a nice word for 'slave.' If a witch binds another's magic, she controls them. So runs traditional witch society."

"All your base are belong to us," I muttered.

Lauren raised an eyebrow. "I guess. Although it's more like a high school clique than Zero Wing. A feral thrall equals big-time popularity points."

"Lucky me," I said.

She frowned. "I'm betting her familiar tagged you. You said she has a cat?" Lauren rolled her eyes. "It's probably black and has some unoriginal name like Greymalkin."

"Isis."

"Uh huh. So yeah, straightforward spell, straightforward counterspell. You have to confront her like Foxy said."

"Why?"

"Because that," Lauren pointed at the trapped curse, "is a psychic parasite. Uninspired but nasty—fangs for rending thoughts, claws for tearing resolve, blah blah blah. It eats the thinking part of your brain, then it propels you to its maker. Voila, one thrall. You have to send it back to its summoner to be rid of it."

I shuddered. "I'm opposed to brain eating, so explain this confronting thing."

"Easy smeasy. Well, maybe less on the easy and more on the smeasy, but essentially, all you have to do is take the curse to Megan. If she wants you back, and she will, she'll ask you to obey her three times. Don't."

"That's it?"

"She won't make it easy for you to say no." She handed me the spaghetti container. "I've imbued the duct tape with virtue. It's sealed against malice and mayhem, but you can open it, Luke."

At my uncomprehending expression, Lauren winked. "'It has a light side and a dark side, and it binds the universe together.'"

I chortled. Weird curse and witchcraft aside, this girl was wicked geeky, a trait I admired.

"Pay attention, genius. You have to tell her three times you deny her and she has no power over you. Then release the curse. It should go for her, your cue to run away, quick as a bunny."

"Confront, deny, run away. Check."

She scooped up Koushee. "Now kiss him on the nose."

"Uh." I'd have preferred kissing Lauren.

"So he knows to watch out for you, because I like you."

Oh hell. I kissed the skunk.

MEGAN'S APARTMENT WAS only a few blocks from the bus stop, but by the time I trudged to it, my backpack with the spaghetti container felt heavier than a semester's worth of textbooks.

I didn't notice anything on the stairs, but outside her door I smelled mold and an undercurrent of ammonia.

I knocked.

When the door opened, all traces of ammonia whisked away, replaced by peaches and cloves.

Megan looked as luscious as she smelled. The tight, low-ride jeans hugged the curve of her hips, and the white, button-down blouse clung to her breasts. Her golden hair curled around her shoulders with a playful bounce that made me think of other pieces of jiggling anatomy.

"Derek."

"May I come in?"

Megan stepped aside, brushing past me to lounge on her sofa. "Have a seat," she said.

She smelled so good, like ripe, spiced fruit, I wanted to bury my face in her hair. It took all my willpower to stay upright.

"I'm not sticking around," I said.

She pouted, her big, cornflower blue eyes winsome. The delicate aroma of bruised aloe drifted up, tugging me to her side. At least I kept on my feet.

"What's your hurry?" She smiled, flashing cherubic dimples. "Hasty words were said, unfortunate words."

Her fingers drifted to the top button of her blouse. Red musk and freshly turned earth. "Didn't we have fun?" The button parted to reveal the shelf of her bra.

I swallowed. "Yeah."

I let her take my hand and lift it to the next button. It unfastened at my touch.

"Undress me, Derek."

I was going for her bra hook when I realized what was happening. *Undress me*, she'd said, and here I was, obeying her like I was already thralled.

I recoiled. "I-I'm just here to return something." Trying to rein in the shakes, I jerked open my backpack and grabbed the spaghetti container. The curse hissed through the plastic.

Megan gasped. The gasp turned into a squawk, and she fell over, writhing and twitching.

"Derek." Her voice was strangled, like she was forcing words through a constricting throat. "Call 911."

My pretty-girl-in-distress reflex activated, and I raced for the phone. I had it off the cradle and my finger on the 9 when the stink enveloped me. Fresh skunk. I've never been sprayed, only experienced it in passing from skunk-dog confrontations or the occasional skunk-car meet up. This was worse. Much worse. My eyes streamed with tears.

"Derek, hurry!"

What was a skunk doing in Megan's apartment? I hit the 1. Had Koushee followed me? But Lauren said he was de-scented.

I was a fingertip away from hitting the last 1 when I caught on. *Call 911* was a command as much as *undress me* had been. I slammed the phone down and swiveled around.

"You'll survive." I inhaled, and the skunk stench was gone.

Megan's transformation was sudden and scary. She glared, all pretense of medical crisis abandoned. "You little prick! This time I won't be so nice. I'll have you cleaning my toilet with your tongue. Isis!"

Megan's black Persian materialized and bounded into her mistress's waiting arms.

"*Exaudite maledictum meam*," Megan intoned.

Isis's eyes glowed amber. The reek of burning tar and smoldering ashes hit me.

"Crap, crap, crap." I fumbled with the Tupperware container. The tape resisted, twisting and stretching.

"*Sisters of darkness, heed me*." Megan's eyes were taking on the same color and illumination as her cat's.

"I deny you, Megan," I said. "You have no power over me."

"*Vindico juvenem*—"

"I deny you, Megan," I babbled, the words tumbling out. "You have no power over me."

My fingernails caught an edge of folded tape. I ripped, and the top came off with a sound like an imploding vacuum.

"*I call upon blight and desolation*—"

I threw the spaghetti container at her, curse and all, and bolted for the door. "I deny you, Megan," I shouted over my shoulder. "Youhavenopoweroverme!"

I spilled into the hall.

Behind me, Megan shrieked. There was a liquid noise, wet paper tearing. My mouth filled with the stench of sulfur. I lunged for the stairwell. A tendril of hot copper curled down my throat, but as I charged down the stairs, it dissipated as fast as the skunk musk had.

When I burst outside, all I could smell was sunshine and sky. I staggered away, quick as a gimpy bunny, and hoped my heart would quit trying to burst out of my chest. It slowed, eventually, and I headed back to Lauren's.

AS SOON AS I pressed the doorbell, a bouquet of wild berries and juniper hit me. Lauren appeared a moment later and ushered me in.

"How'd it go?" She plopped onto her futon.

"The opposite of easy smeasy. She almost got me with the last one. Except a skunk happened to spray just then, and it shocked my head clear."

"A skunk—?"

Koushee, on cue, popped out from under the futon.

"Oh, he *did* help you!" Lauren scooped him up. "What a good boy," she cooed. "Who's a clever skunk? Kooshee is, yes, he is."

I cleared my throat. "Lauren, is there's something important about threes?"

"Yepper. It's a whole big mystic foundation."

"When I was here, you asked me to do three things."

"Did I?"

"Get the duct tape, finish my tea, and kiss your skunk on the nose."

"So?"

"And I *imbibed* something you brewed."

Lauren studied me from behind a pair of round, skunk ears. "You think I cursed you?"

"Did you?"

She cuddled Kooshee. "The thing about familiars, they're faithful and steadfast unto death, the best allies, but they're also all instinct and impulse. Koushee knows I need a bigger magical arsenal in order to maintain my autonomy; however, he can't grasp concepts like term papers and flunking out of school. He hooked us together in his own, simplistic way because he sensed you could be useful to me. But I'm *not* a traditionalist. I don't curse or thrall people. My friends and lovers support me because they want to and because they know they can count on me to do the same."

I flushed when she said *lovers*.

"I did dose your tea with a tranquility spell, but only because I didn't want you to freak when I went prospecting for curses."

Koushee purr-oinked as Lauren rubbed his head.

"So what happens if I deny you three times?"

"Go ahead, if it'll make you feel better."

I did, but my heart wasn't in it. Nothing happened except Koushee's whiskers quivered in what I was betting was the equivalent of a skunk laugh.

"If you want," Lauren said, "you can take off, go your own way, and I'll go mine. No harm, no foul."

"And if I stay?"

"Then I teach you about magic, and we become allies."

"What kind of allies?" My voice ended in a squeak, ruining my attempt at nonchalance.

Lauren set the skunk down. "That depends." Her hair smelled like pomegranates. "What kind do you want to be?" She kissed me, and her lips tasted like magic.

Koushee trotted away, thoughtfully giving us some privacy.

"A Nose for Magic" was a finalist for the 2007 Pagan Fiction Award. Yes, I have skunks on the brain. But I still think a skunk would make a kick-ass familiar, better by far than a cat. In my experience, skunks are phenomenally intuitive and astonishingly clever, possessing the ability to bend two reasonably intelligent adult humans to their will with very little effort. Or maybe I'm just deluding myself with the "reasonably intelligent" part.

THE CENTER OF THE UNIVERSE

WITH A CLASS size of seventy-two, my high school reunions were more like family get-togethers. The class of '83 was a demoralizing family though, filled with peers like distant cousins who knew me when I was gawky and spastic, excruciatingly self-conscious in my metamorphosing skin. I'd avoided them—classmates, reunions, my estranged family—easy to do when I lived four states away. But, like with other family gatherings, it was death that brought me back home to my twenty-year reunion: Marc's funeral.

His mother, a woman I remembered as an intensely assertive homemaker, had phoned me three days ago. They'd found him on some quiet side road, a 9mm bullet propelled at high velocity through his brain. Nothing missing, no signs of struggle, but no gun either. A stumper to the fine officers of Concorde, Indiana, and a nagging riddle to me. But I'd finally learned that I couldn't solve every riddle.

I hadn't spoken to Marc in over five years, our communications limited to vacuous holiday cards and

Spartan emails. Another page of my past turning over, I was set to observe it without even a cursory bookmarking. But as I searched for a sympathy card in my cluttered home office, I stumbled across the small, stuffed bear Marc had won for me at a county fair once upon a time. I wasn't prone to superstitious fancies, but it made me nostalgic. Didn't I owe Marc this last goodbye?

Still, I couldn't help feeling exasperated as I booked my flight that he'd chosen this, of all times, to get himself killed.

Reunion evening, seeing Natalie again didn't bother me as much as I'd expected. I suppose it really couldn't have; I'd have suffered a dual aneurysm and stroke if it had.

Natalie had been my first true love affair. She'd been eighteen, I a precocious seventeen. We started out best friends as freshmen, our lockers next to each other. With my mother all but certifiable and Natalie's greater age and world experience, she became my mentor, confidante, lover, and yes, even mother-figure.

How I adored her.

I'd only recently been able to admit to myself that I'd never gotten over her, never been able to move on despite a string of girlfriends, lovers, and even a life-partner. In the end it was always the same; they couldn't measure up to the standard Natalie had set over two decades ago.

I hesitated in the doorway. Natalie had her back to me. She'd gotten fat. Not just fat, obese. She wore a sleeveless black dress with a tiger batiked on the hem. A longer, cheetah-print underskirt completed the jungle motif. It wasn't flattering. Her arms were exposed from wrist to shoulder, white and doughy with dimples that framed her elbows.

It was petty, the relief I felt. A part of me had expected her to be unchanged. Though she had never been willowy, her figure had been lush and ripe, supple without being flabby.

Her hair was short too, cut below her ears. I'd always liked it long—the stream of relentlessly straight chestnut-brown fanning out behind her on a pillow or as a shimmering curtain at her back. She had taken to wearing it short after graduation.

Bethany Campbell spied me lurking in the shadows.

"Kimberly! Kimberly Harris, isn't it? I'm so glad you could make it."

She grasped my hand, half to pump it, half to tug me into the old student lounge. "You look exactly the same! I wouldn't believe it's been twenty years." She handed me a self-adhesive nametag and a blue marker.

"Thanks." She was being kind. Despite monthly trips to the salon to re-tint gray roots, annual whitening touch-ups at the dentist, weekly yoga, aerobics, and step classes to keep the thickening waistline and slowing metabolism in check, I looked my age.

I scribbled out my name and plastered the sunny label to my suit jacket.

"We missed you at the other reunions," Bethany continued.

"I moved out of state."

"I'm glad you could make it this year."

"I'm in town for a funeral."

"Oh." Bethany's cheerful patter died away, which

had been my intention. I liked her, but we'd never been close. Now she reminded me of a cheek-pinching aunt with her garrulous small talk and overbearing friendliness.

"I'll let you mingle," she said. "There's soda and wine."

"Thanks."

Bethany pulled me into a fierce hug. "I'm really glad you could make it."

It rocked me, this impulsive touch. Since Faye and I had split, I had drifted in an orbit of remote acquaintances and standoffish co-workers. I couldn't remember the last time anyone had hugged me.

Off-balance, I wasn't ready for Natalie to turn around. The line of her nose had elongated and widened, becoming beaky where it had been distinctive. The tapered curve of her chin submerged into puffy flesh bulging under her jaw. And her eyes were huge, brown pools behind wire-rimmed glasses. I'd never been able to convince her to try contacts. In her eyes I saw the young beauty I remembered, lost in the folds and flab of a clumsily aging body.

"Kimi," she said. "I didn't know you were coming."

Neither of us moved. In high school, Natalie had shown me with her easy exuberance how to take joy in casual touches: friendly hugs and linked arms. Now we couldn't even shake hands.

"Marc was my friend too," I said.

"I didn't mean it that way. It's just you haven't been to the last two reunions—"

"I live in New Jersey," I said. "It's not exactly a ten-minute drive like it is for you."

"Concorde is a good place to live." Such

belligerence in those words. Like old times.

How often had she railed against Concorde and filled afternoons with dreams of escaping the sleepy town to ports bigger and wilder? "I won't die in the same place I was born," she'd vowed. And here she was, securely established in Concorde, while I was the one who had broken free.

But I wasn't there to pick a fight. "Concorde is a nice town," I said. "I've lived in worse."

Maybe she didn't want to fight either."What have you been up to?" she asked. "Haven't heard from you in forever."

I shrugged. "I got my MA in Psychology and then dumped the whole thing when IBM offered me a job as a systems analyst."

"How did that come about? I thought you were really into psych."

"I was. Still am. People, motivation, behavior—it's all fascinating. I got tired of the politics and games at the university. Didn't think I could stand it for another two years to get my doctorate. Started taking some programming classes instead. The pay is good, even with the IT bust."

She nodded. "Yeah, my degree turned out pretty useless too."

"What was it again? Global Justice and Strategic Studies or something like that?"

"Global Peace and Strategies, yes."

"I never understood what that curriculum was about."

"Neither did the people I sent my resume to." She laughed, a rueful, good-natured bray. "Basically it was Economics, Sociology, and Poli-Sci all bundled together, with a big dollop of cultural philosophy tossed in. Now I answer phones and help Luddites print their email. In the name of global peace, of course."

I grinned. "Of course. You still living with Eliot?"

"Actually, we got married."

Obviously, I hadn't been invited to the celebration of their union, although I was irrationally hurt I hadn't even received an announcement. But Natalie had called marriage a worthless institution. She hadn't come to the commitment ceremony Faye and I'd had, but then she hadn't approved of Faye either. Another something to let go of.

"It was a real shock getting that call from Marc's mom," I said. "I'm astonished she even had my number."

"She asked me for it." Natalie chewed her lip, a habit she had when she was feeling uncomfortable or guilty. She wouldn't look at me either, her eyes drifting over my right shoulder towards the buffet table. I recalled a bit of trivia from psychology class: most people looked leftward when they engaged the creative hemisphere of their brain—fantasy, imagination, and lies.

What was the lie? That Natalie had asked Marc's mother to call me? That would be like her, too proud to reach out to me and pressuring someone else to do it.

"She was pretty incoherent when we spoke," I said. "I didn't want to ask for details. What happened?"

"No one's sure."

"The police don't have any leads or suspects or anything?"

"Not without the gun. They looked for it, but you

know how the Concorde cops are."

They'd been the butt of many teenage jokes. "I can't believe they're still such fuck-ups."

"Believe it. And get this, the police came around our place and grilled Eliot and me for a couple hours."

"You're kidding. They thought you had something to do with Marc's shooting?"

"Not really," she shrugged, "But they freaked us out and got off on it. You know how it is."

And I did. I laughed at the absurdity of it; I couldn't help myself. "You thought they were busting you for drugs?"

She pressed her lips together, furious. "You haven't changed a bit. You're still a spiteful bitch." Natalie spun away, striding to the buffet with quick, jerky steps. She filled her plate with pastries and chips.

I had no enthusiasm for the rest of the reunion. I made my rounds, spoke to old classmates, met their spouses and children, and left.

Our high school had been on the border of the university campus. A laboratory school, it shared many of the facilities and resources of the big, state university, including a preponderance of cheap hotels.

My hotel room was bright and loud, the raucous sounds across the hall bleeding through the cardboard-thin walls and the lights from the parking lot seeping through the flimsy curtains. Last year's hit movies didn't interest me, nor the piped-in nudie videos.

I put on jeans and a loose sweater. Blue and violet, dark colors, bruise colors. They suited my mood.

My rental car grumbled to life in the chilly October

air. I didn't bother with map or destination. I couldn't get lost in Concorde. I'd grown up here, ridden my bike through the streets and thoroughfares, hiked barefoot through backyards and golf courses, and clamored over fences and walls.

I circled the university campus, doing grit laps up Main Street, across College, down Center, and over University. The height of weekend entertainment, townies and students alike driving in circles, stopping in the middle of the road to gossip and giggle with a cavalier disregard for stoplights and traffic laws.

Phantom voices: Natalie and Eliot in the backseat, hitting off a fat joint before passing it to Marc, riding shotgun. Marc furtively waving the smoke out the window before passing the toke to me at a red light. Looping around campus in a giggly haze. And when I was too high to drive anymore, pulling into the parking lot of the Museum of Natural History.

I found myself in that barren lot, the single streetlight casting more shadows than illumination on the old, brick and stone building. The heater wafted hot, dry air over me, comforting as happy memories.

This had been our favorite hangout place, away from parents, safe and clandestine. We came here to get stoned, come down, make out, but most of all, to be together. We'd called it the *Center of the Universe.*

I turned off the ignition and got out. There was only one way into the Center of the Universe. I slung my purse over my shoulder, better to free my hands.

The fire escape ladder was overhead, out of reach, but not the diagonal wall support. I jumped, grabbed hold, and half-shimmied, half-swung myself up. I'd done this in stiletto heels, drunk and high, and a couple of times tripping on LSD or 'shrooms. I wasn't young anymore, but I remembered. The riskiest section was the first part; you were the most exposed. After you reached the ladder, the shadows and the foliage protected you from random passersby, or less random campus police.

I scaled the rungs, pausing halfway at the second floor landing. Four stories in all, not a great distance unless you were climbing the outside of a building, supported only by slender metal bars.

It was so ingrained it felt like instinct: don't look down, never look down.

I was afraid of heights. Yet, up I went, guarded by the spreading oak tree, its leaves still abundant this early in autumn. I'd had to conquer my fear every time.

At the top, another moment of exposure as I slipped over the ledge. Then the walls were guardian, shield, and sanctuary.

Above me was exhilaration. I remembered this sky, the clear, crisp vista from the roof. I'd seen it lying on my back on blankets smuggled from home, watched the sunsets, the stars, the moon. I'd gotten high beneath this sky, made love beneath it, and been happy once, all under that vast openness.

On winter nights, when there was snow or frigid chill, or when we were too buzzed to climb back down, there was the attic, a little storage area with stark, wooden studs interspersed with insulation. We had to duck our heads or get tangled in cobwebs. Eliot, with his six foot two inches, once banged his skull on the slanted whitewall hard enough to bring down a rain of debris.

It was the heart of the Center of the Universe.

The metal door creaked when I pulled on it. The

university hadn't fixed the lock. Did they even know the door, this attic, existed? It opened to familiar darkness, windowless and deep.

I stepped in, letting the door close behind me as I breathed the musty air. Dust, mold, old beer, and pot smoke, just as I remembered it.

In the darkness, I only knew my eyes were open by the absence of eyelashes brushing my cheeks. It was a comfortable pressure, familiar as a tatty flannel shirt. Memories like shadow shapes grew out of the emptiness, spurred by the familiar scents.

I envisioned the catwalk that led to an alcove. Marathon Dungeons and Dragons tournaments there, the silence broken by faint strains of music from Natalie's boombox: The Police, INXS, Depeche Mode, U2. Conjured by memory, the wailing guitar opening of "Synchronicity II" throbbed, punctuated by the clatter of plastic dice. We'd hung blankets like curtains and piled sleeping bags stolen from the storage closets and basements of our parents on the wooden floor. Milk crates swiped and furtively lugged up for tables and a few ragged throw pillows completed our nesting. It was drafty in winter and sweltering in summer, but it was ours, our Center of the Universe.

For light, we'd bought a candelabra at Big Lots and filled it with rainbow-hued candles. In retrospect, it was probably a miracle we hadn't burned the place down. Eliot stored his bong here, enshrined in its own milk crate with various drug fixings: balloons and dispensers for nitrous, lighters, chips and gum for the inevitable munchies.

I had my first real kiss here. Marc and I, fumbling to Led Zeppelin's "Stairway to Heaven."

Marc had been my oldest friend—red-haired, freckled, and lanky. We met in third grade after I transferred in from a different district. It was an age when boys lost status in their mysterious schoolyard hierarchy if they were seen fraternizing with girls, and girls were cruel and malicious to newcomers who read books and disdained polo shirts and designer sneakers. By third grade, cliques were carved in granite with pecking orders fixed as eternity. I was a tomboy and an outsider, immediately branded a freak, destined for years of solitary elementary school hell.

Until I met Marc. He had four older sisters and was oblivious to the stigma of girl cooties. Best of all, he shared my fascination with Star Wars and Middle-Earth, spaceships and dragons.

Marc had been my best friend. We stuck together, even after I moved in sixth grade and had to transfer to another district. Then, in high school, I met Natalie and Eliot. Marc had reservations when I invited them to our Saturday gaming sessions. So I was delighted when Natalie and Marc hit it off so well. But also a bit resentful, jealous even.

Those uncomfortable feelings of insecurity had spurred me to kiss him during a stolen moment, just Marc and I, romantically lit by candlelight. I hadn't loved him, not that way. I loved him as my closest friend, the boy I'd grown up with, but not as a boyfriend, a lover. The kiss was awkward and messy—a banging of teeth, tongues everywhere, noses in the way. After that, our friendship took on a new, uncomfortable intimacy.

We submerged in each other, lost in the novelty of it. I enjoyed the attention, but it always felt forced, unnatural. It wasn't until years later that I understood why.

Natalie was the first person I told, and she astonished me by bursting into tears. Our first friction, mended when she and Eliot began dating.

The summer of our senior year, my mother found the pot and the half-empty packet of contraceptive pills in my backpack. In the fallout, I ran away, and Natalie went with me. Solidarity. We didn't run far. In the candlelit shadows of the Center of the Universe, giggling to cover our dismay, I realized I loved Natalie, truly loved her, the way I didn't love Marc. I kissed her, and wondrous of wonders, she kissed me back. We made love on the tattered sleeping bags.

Marc found us that evening, both of us blinking at his flashlight, our eyes dilated from the dark when the candles burned away. Before Natalie or I could speak, he dropped the flashlight and fled.

Accusations and recriminations followed. We all made up, although it was never the same after that.

Closing my eyes, I remembered Marc's thin smile, the way he used to hum when he didn't know what to say. Instead of dust and mold, I smelled the Dial soap he always used. How could he be gone?

"Oh, Marc," I whispered. "What happened to you?"

"I was waiting. I knew I could count on you."

I blinked. Marc stood there, luminous in the darkness. He wore corduroy pants, the cuffs frayed and the knees worn threadbare. He'd always hated jeans. And he had on his favorite shirt, the one with the African weave and the flared sleeves.

Except how could I see him in the darkness, without candle or flashlight? And he was dead, gunshot-wound-to-the-head dead.

I turned away, frightened, groping for the box of matches stored under the strut beside the lintel. I forgot that over a decade had passed since this had been my home away from home.

"Kimi, don't you want to help me?"

No matches, of course. It was an alien claustrophobia, the darkness pressing at my back. Marc waited for me to turn and confront his ghost, or admit I was going mad. Paragraphs from my Abnormal Psych. textbooks: trauma from grief and mourning, psychotic triggers.

I groped along the wall, frantic to find the doorknob. My hand hit a metal box. With a switch. I flicked it, and three dim bulbs lit, sluicing the attic with comforting incandescence.

"They installed lights while you've been gone."

I yelped.

"Sorry if I startled you."

My heart still lurched in my chest, but I was no longer terrified. "Eliot?"

"Natalie said you were at the reunion. I wondered if you'd end up here."

Eliot stepped out of my memories and the shadows that lined the catwalk. He hadn't changed as much as Natalie. His hair remained long, past his shoulders in a riot of tight curls. If it was thinning and more limp than wild, I overlooked it. He was heavier too, in his face and gut. But it was Eliot. In the reality of his presence, I convinced myself that Marc's apparition had been my imagination, maybe the wine I'd drunk.

"You look good, Eliot. I was hoping to get a chance to catch up with you this weekend. Didn't expect it to be here, though."

His grin was tentative, front teeth bunched together and crooked. The acne scars on his face were stark in the harsh light. "Aside from the lights, they also paneled and painted the walls. 'Course, our stuff is gone."

"Who cleared it out?" When we'd splintered, I stopped going to the hangout, abandoning the dog-eared copies of my Elfquest graphic novels and my TSR *Player's Handbook* with regret.

"Nat grabbed some stuff. She came up for my bong and stash, dragged down her parents' old sleeping bag. When she left for college, I kept meaning to come back to dismantle the rest but never did. We came on her Christmas break, but the place was trashed—the candelabra smashed apart, the posters shredded. The scrapbook, you remember the one we filled with pictures of us and our writing? It was torn to bits. She thought it was you."

"You thought I'd want to wreck it? Why?" I'd always assumed one of them had retrieved the album, at least.

"Nat wouldn't talk about what happened between you two."

"You could've asked me."

Eliot shrugged. "Wouldn't have mattered anyway. It was done."

It always irritated me—in the end, infuriated me—Eliot's passive aggression.

"It wasn't me," I said.

"I'm glad."

We exchanged smiles.

"Hey, you want to come back to the house? Have a beer and a toke, like old times?"

Did I? Yes, I did. But—

"Nat and I had a bit of a clash at the reunion," I said. "Not sure if she'd welcome me."

"It's my home too." That surprised me. Eliot always kowtowed to Natalie. Another exasperation, how she manipulated him and took his submission for granted. "Besides, she told me about it. I could tell she felt sort of bad."

That was more like Eliot.

"Where are you parked?" I asked. "I've got a rental in the museum lot."

"I didn't drive. We live in the same house. I walked."

We left through the inside of the museum. The door in the middle of the catwalk only locked going into the attic. From within, the knob turned easily, leading to an echoing stairwell. We'd propped the door open to smuggle in the larger furnishings, things we couldn't lug up in backpacks. That door and those stairs had probably saved us from injury or other tragedy, giving us a safe alternative to scaling the outside fire escape drunk or stoned, in snow and thunderstorm.

Eliot flipped the shiny, new switch as we left.

The drive was short. I'd been to their house once, a place they'd moved into after Nat returned from college. Eliot directed me to the slanted driveway.

It was as I remembered it, with its front lawn overgrown and a pair of bicycles leaning against the porch. It wanted a paint job and a good cleaning. But then, who was I to pass judgment? I hated housework, paid a set of women to vacuum and dust and had a guy come round when the grass got too long. If my Nazi homeowners association hadn't griped about it, my place would probably look as unkempt as Eliot and Natalie's.

The porch was raggedly screened, and spiders spun their webs among the dim light fixtures. The front door squeaked.

"Nat," Eliot called, "guess who I found at the Center of the Universe?"

He led me past the kitchen and into the living room. I recognized the sofa from Natalie's parents, the futon from Eliot's old apartment. The stereo was new though, a cluster of polished, black components on a rickety shelving unit. Peter Gabriel's *Passion* murmured from the speakers. Candles illuminated the room in mirrored wall sconces and a bright cluster on the coffee table. The burning nib of an incense stick wafted patchouli-scented smoke to mingle with the haze of an elusive, troublesome sense of déjà vu.

Natalie had Eliot's bong in hand, the same black cylinder with the jutting pipe bowl from high school. It even had the same Grateful Dead sticker on it, although the brilliant reds and blues were faded, muted by time and handling. She exhaled a stream of blue smoke.

"Hi, Kimi." She handed Eliot the bong and a plastic lighter. "Have a seat, have a toke. Help yourself to anything in the 'fridge."

We were back to a truce. I liberated a Samuel Adams from the kitchen and snagged an extra for Eliot.

In the living room, Eliot's cheeks puffed out like a chipmunk's as he held smoke and breath. We traded bong for bottle, and I sat across from them on the futon.

I hadn't lit up since college, another contentious topic between Natalie and me. She'd taken my abstemiousness as a personal criticism of her habit. My personal choices offending her when they differed from her own was the last in a long series of wedges between us.

A lungful of smoke seemed a small price to keep the peace.

Eliot lifted his bottle. "To Marc, happy trails wherever you are, buddy."

We clinked bottles.

The pot made another round. I had become a lightweight. Two hits left me detached, hovering with an analytical air in the space above my body. This was why I'd stopped smoking. I hated that padding in my head, the barrier that made it hard to think. It also scoured my throat raw, despite the cooling length of bong.

"So what did the police ask you?" I heard myself say.

Eliot took another swig of beer and avoided my gaze.

Natalie capped the bowl, snuffing out the red ember to conserve leaf.

"Can't you let it go?" she said.

"Doesn't it bug you not knowing what happened?"

She scowled. "The night he died, we got into a fight," she said. "About you."

"Me? But I haven't talked to Marc in years. We exchanged Christmas cards and stuff, but I haven't seen him for nearly as long as—"

"As long as you haven't seen us," Eliot finished. He'd always had an unnerving tendency of finishing our sentences, Natalie's and mine, especially when we were all high.

"I thought you guys stayed close," I said.

"We did," Natalie said. "We hung out all the time. Most evenings Marc came over and we chilled."

The déjà vu, formless and ambiguous before, intensified, goaded alive by the alcohol and THC. The darkness, the music, the intimacy, and now the shared inebriation. This place felt like the Center of the Universe. Natalie and Eliot had remade our sanctuary. There was only one thing missing.

As though I conjured him with my thoughts, Marc materialized beside me, seated with ankles crossed. He reached for the bong and sucked up a lungful of smoke through the bubbling water.

Neither Natalie nor Eliot responded, and the pot made his apparition soothing instead of upsetting. I'd had my share of drug-induced hallucinations; one more wasn't going to faze me, even one of Marc.

"We fought," Marc said, "Natalie and me. I wanted her to invite you down for the reunion. Thought it was well past time to patch things up."

"Nat didn't want to call me, did she? And you pressed her."

"Not me," Eliot said, "Marc."

I didn't correct him.

"He really missed you," Eliot continued. "Whenever we got together for holidays, he mentioned you."

Marc nodded, smoke issuing from his nostrils. "Ask them if they missed you."

I started to, but chickened out. "Do you ever wish for the old days?"

"Do you?" Nat's tone was less languid than mine.

"I did for a long time. Then I moved on." I was lying. "Faye, my ex-, you never gave her a chance. We were good. You never saw it. I used to wish you had.

She was really good for me, taught me a lot about myself, about living." I was babbling. Another effect of the pot.

"You broke up," Nat said. "Guess she stopped being good for you."

The bludgeon of her voice hurt. Defensive hackles lifted, old habits. But I wasn't seventeen anymore. Faye had been more than good for me; she'd been healthy, the healthiest relationship I'd ever had. And what she'd taught me about honesty and openness revealed the truth to my pot-addled mind. Natalie had been jealous of Faye.

"It was me that wasn't good for her," I said. "I criticized her all the time, couldn't stop myself. Seemed like no matter what, she couldn't make me happy. So I called it quits."

Marc nodded. "It was for the best."

"I figured she'd be better off without me."

Natalie reached for her beer, clung to the glass. Her hands shook as she tipped it to her mouth. "I'm sorry."

I'd never heard her apologize. In all the years we spent together—weekends, summer holidays, and sleepovers—not once had Natalie admitted fault for anything.

"What are you sorry for?" Eliot asked.

"I used to get on Kimi about everything," she said.

I gulped some beer and discovered I'd finished the bottle. "You were right, most of the time," I said. "It was your grilling that got me questioning and thinking. I'd be a devout Jesusfreak, probably pregnant with a dozen kids, popping antidepressants, and wondering what the hell was wrong with me if you hadn't got me out of that rut."

"Eliot and I went to marriage counseling, y'know. The therapist told me I had self-esteem issues."

"We all did," I said. "We were in high school."

"I harp on Eliot like I did you. It made me, *makes* me, feel better."

The Natalie I'd known would have given up teeth, eyes, and tongue before admitting that.

"I wish you could've said that a long time ago," I said. "I wish we could go back and fix what happened."

"At last," Marc sighed. "I've been waiting for so long."

The tangled ropes of smoke thickened, turning murky and heavy. The tendrils of pot congealed against my face. They strangled the candles, dimming the yellow of their light to brassy shadows. The ringlets of smoke transformed into soft arms wrapping me close, holding me. Years dissolved away, and the forgotten, suddenly remembered, feel of a woman's lips pressed against my mouth. Natalie's tongue was dry against mine, rasping in our shared cottonmouth. I giggled and she tweaked my nipple. It was too much. I burst into peals of laughter, tipping backward to flop on the pile of sleeping bags. Distantly, I knew I should've been troubled, but recollections of futons in living rooms became misty and vague, like a dreamscape or a remembered LSD trip.

"I love you, you ninny," Natalie said.

"I know, I know," I said, gasping to catch my breath. "I love you too."

"We'll always be together won't we, Kimi? All of us, Eliot and Marc too. After we graduate, we'll get a farmhouse, live off the land and off the grid."

"I want nothing more." The solemnity of the moment chased away the giggles. This was our dream, move away from it all, start a commune, be free and happy, and most important of all, together.

Sweaty and peaceful, we lay entwined, my head nestled on her breasts, her arm draped across my hip. Sleep tugged at my eyelids, although I knew if I surrendered to it, I would wake to Marc's flashlight and the beginning of our estrangement. As consciousness reeled away, I wondered how I knew.

I HEARD MARC'S footsteps on the catwalk. The blanket-curtain parted. But it wasn't one beam that sprang through it, but two. Marc had brought Eliot.

That wasn't right; it wasn't how it had happened. As the thought surfaced, it faded. Going. Gone.

I sat, clutching a fold of sleeping bag to my chest.

Eliot's face was a mask of shock, consternation. Marc's wasn't. There wasn't a trace of surprise to crease his brow or drop his jaw.

Beside me, Natalie stirred.

"Mind if we join you?" Marc's question was somber, deadly serious.

Natalie smiled and cuddled my hip. "Take off your shoes first."

I relaxed, releasing the breath I'd been holding. "You heard her," I said. "Off with your shoes."

Inhibitions were tossed aside, left with the shoes and clothing kicked outside the blanket curtain. Sometime during the day, Marc refreshed the candelabra with new candles so we might see which hand pressed against whose flesh, know who we kissed before we felt and tasted lips and tongue. Breathless and panting, we parted so Natalie could switch on her boombox.

Marc said it even as I thought it. "I wish it could always be like this."

"Me too," Eliot said.

"It will be," Natalie said. "I'll always love all of you. We should live together like I was saying to Kimi."

"We're growing apart," Marc said. "You and Kimi are going to different colleges. I'm staying here for university, and Eliot—"

"I'm not even going to college," Eliot said.

"This is the best it will ever be."

"Don't say that," Natalie said. "Of course we'll change, in good ways. How could anything come between us?"

But the mood was broken. We assembled our clothes as Eliot rolled a joint by glimmering candleshine. On an impulse, I shouldered the topmost sleeping bag. We emerged from the Center of the Universe to discover the sun had set as we loved. A slender sickle of moon gleamed, waited upon by a smattering of stars.

I flung the sleeping bag on the fire escape ledge, the best view of sky and campus skyline. We sat close but not touching, passing the smoldering joint from hand to hand.

"Why can't we stay like this?" There was resentment and grief in Natalie's question.

"People change," I said with my new, mysterious wisdom.

"There *is* a way to stay here and now," Marc said. He stood, his arms wide as though to embrace the night.

"Get down," I said. "Someone'll see you."

"Stay with me," Marc said. "Promise you'll stay with me."

Before any of us could stop him, he jumped, flinging himself into empty space. For a moment, he seemed to hover, as though unsure whether to float or drop. Gravity decided for him. His body crashed through leaves and air.

"Marc!" It was only four stories. He could still be alive. I put my hand on the fire escape ladder and made the mistake of looking. The world tipped and spun, sending me gasping to my knees.

Behind me, Natalie and Eliot rose, a hairbreadth slower to react.

"We have to call 911," I panted. "Not too late. It can't be."

Natalie gazed down, unaffected by my phobia. She reached back. "Eliot?"

Eliot took her hand, their faces the same in that eerie, psychic way Eliot had. "Yes."

"Do you love me?"

"Always."

"I love you. You and Marc and Kimi."

She held her hand out to me. "C'mon."

The belief, the love on their faces.

I gripped her hand, hard, like I would never let go. Together, we stood on the ledge. Four stories below, Marc waited for us.

"On three?" Natalie said.

"On three," Eliot agreed.

"One."

"This is better, isn't it?" I said. "Better than growing apart and hating each other."

"I could never hate you," Natalie said.

"Two."

"Yes you could."

"Don't be stupid."

"Three!"

Eliot launched himself over, dragging Natalie halfway, their hands clasped tight. In that second of sundered faith, I threw myself flat and gripped the fire escape's support.

Natalie screamed.

We straggled out, flung dangerously over the precipice; Eliot committed to the air, anchored only by Natalie's tenuous hold. My shoulder burned, wrenched and agonized. Her hand slipped in mine.

"Don't let go," she pleaded.

"I never did." I was losing my grip, sliding from the metal support.

"Eliot, can you reach a branch?" I shouted.

"It's too far!"

Natalie screamed again. I felt them shift, a dead weight on my arm. If I let go, we would all fall. All together, forever, as Marc had wanted.

I looked into Natalie's red and frightened face. Below her, Eliot dangled, pale and limp.

I let go.

Clinging to the strut of fire escape, I watched them fall away. Vertigo twisted the world into sickening colors and sounds. I clenched my eyes shut and clutched the metal bars.

"YOU DIDN'T COME with us." Marc sat beside me, his fingers toying with the mouth of Eliot's bong. Although I knew Marc was the ghost, it was the black plastic that looked translucent. "I waited for you, but you never came."

The queasy dizziness was gone, replaced with a

sober calmness and a certainty granted by facets of Marc's personality I'd come to understand only now, after his death.

"How come you wrecked the picture album?" I asked. "We made it together."

He scowled. "It was a lie. All those promises, those happy, smiling faces."

"Ours, you mean."

"I erased the lies."

He'd never gotten over his obsession either, not just with me, but with what we'd had with Natalie and Eliot.

"But you kept waiting," I said. "And when you realized I wasn't coming back, you shot yourself. But why did Natalie take the gun, or was it Eliot?" That was the lie she'd tried to hide, the reason Eliot wouldn't meet my eyes. More than the pot, they hadn't wanted the police to find the *gun*.

His face was intense. "I got you to come back, didn't I?"

"Only to say goodbye."

"Natalie and Eliot are here. We could be together. They understood when I told Eliot to take the gun away, he understood. You would come if there was a question mark. You never could resist a puzzle."

"You can't keep them, Marc."

"Why? Because you want them in spite of everything, even without me?" Was that eagerness in his voice?

"No. Because I *don't* want them. I don't want them or you. And because I don't want them, you can't have any of us."

Marc howled.

I felt only pity when he melted to mist and then

nothingness, the bong slipping from his fingers to spill its dirty, pungent water on the carpet.

I OPENED MY eyes. Across from me, Natalie and Eliot blinked.

"Since Marc's death was a suicide," I said, "I won't tell the cops that the gun's at the Center of the Universe, but you'd better do something with it."

"How'd you—?" Natalie began.

I held up my hand, and she trailed into silence. "Eliot knew about the lights and paneling they put in. I figured he or the both of you had been there recently. Besides, where else would you stash it?"

"We were falling," Eliot said.

"I caught you. But I'm done. You can stand or fall on your own." I left, stepping over the puddle of smoke-infused water seeping into the carpet.

AFTER MARC'S FUNERAL, Eliot and Natalie invited me back to their place. Eliot suggested I stay in their guest room. I declined. Instead, I went back to my hotel, packed up my belongings, and turned in for an early night. I had a flight home the next morning.

My house in New Jersey was quiet and dark when I arrived. The motion-sensitive porch light went on as I climbed the steps. I half expected to see a patina of dust and cobwebs overlaying my familiar possessions—my bookshelves, the television, the dining table. But everything sparkled, cleaning-ladies spotless, just as I'd left it mere days ago.

The number came easily. I hadn't dialed it since the breakup, had erased it from my speed dial, but my fingers remembered.

After the third ring, Faye picked up. "Hello?" She sounded sleepy. I envisioned her hair all disheveled from her pillow.

"It's Kimi."

"Kimi?" In the space of my name, she woke up. "What is it? Is something the matter?" A pause. "Do you know what time it is?"

"Nothing's the matter. I got back from my high school reunion."

"Oh. Uh, how was it?"

"Pretty lame. Much as I expected."

A long silence hung between us. We both tried to end it at the same time.

"Faye—"

"Kimi—"

I forged ahead when she faltered. "I'm sorry."

"Sorry for what?"

"For everything. For the mess I made of our lives."

She surprised me by laughing. "It takes two people to muck up a relationship."

"I know." The newfound resolve I'd found in Concorde was evaporating. "I miss you." It came out in a rush. "I really miss you."

"Moving out was your idea." It wasn't an accusation or reproof, just a flat statement.

"I know."

"Look, I never stopped loving you. You know that, right? I told you that."

"I'm sorry," I whispered.

She sighed, deep and long-suffering. "You want to come over for coffee or something? Have a talk?"

"Yes. Please."

"I'll be here."

"I never stopped loving you either." The words tumbled out, tripping over themselves in my mouth. They weren't romantic or heartfelt, and yet they were. "You weren't waiting for me, were you?"

"No." I heard the smile in her voice. "But I kept hoping."

"The Center of the Universe" received an honorable mention in The Year's Best Science Fiction: Twenty-Fifth Annual Collection, *edited by Gardner Dozois. I wrote it shortly after not attending my 15-year high school reunion and learning of the suicide of an upperclassman, Iris Chang. My high school was tiny, a laboratory school for gifted students with an enrollment of around 300 students spanning five grades. Everyone pretty much knew everyone, and even though I wasn't particularly close to Iris, I was deeply saddened by the tragedy. My high school years were an extremely turbulent as well as formative period of my life—although I guess that's true of almost everyone's high school years—and my memories of how people were and how they've changed since then aren't easily reconciled.*

THE WIZARD OF ETERNAL WATCH

WITHIN THE CASTLE at the end of the world, the wards and enchantments stirred, rousing themselves like heavy beasts emerging from a long winter's sleep. They stretched and glanced about, triggered to alertness by the necessity of waking the next Wizard of Eternal Watch.

Reika felt sleep tugged away. She clung to it like a stubborn child to warm blankets. The dream was so delicious: Zinan in the rain, his arms around her, whispering promises of tomorrow. That had been the day they had fought over their assignments as keeper and wizard. He had called her detached and cold; she had called him thin-skinned and sentimental. From fury to lovemaking, they had proved each accusation untrue with sweet kisses, sharp teeth in flesh, and fiery passion under the weeping sky.

The spells knew how to deal with this too. They invaded her slumbering psyche, replaced her memory of Zinan with words, oaths, promises made. Her voice, her pledges.

Reika's eyes snapped open and the diamond casement floated apart, halving itself where before it had been a single, flawless stone. Released from stasis, she felt a familiar mingling of anticipation and dread.

Zinan would be waiting for her in the Chamber of Command.

She reached for her crown and used it to murmur forth a simple spell that pushed the last veil of Waiting from her thoughts.

The Chamber of Command was the nexus of the castle. There was only one corridor from her quarters, as there was only one corridor from every Waiting quarters, and it led to the Chamber. Like a great beating heart, stone arteries sent wizards and keepers to and fro in a sluggish dance across eternity.

The Chamber had not changed in the years since she had occupied it last. Shimmering images threw ghostly shadows against the smooth, round walls in regular planes of illusion. These were the cages.

Before each panel, a cube, no larger than her head, hovered midair with golden, translucent sides. These were the locks.

The prisoners could be seen, tiny demons fighting, dancing, sleeping within their cubicles.

Reika was a jailor, one of a pair rotated in sets—one Wizard of Eternal Watch and one Keeper of Forever per century—chosen and trained to wield illusion. They harnessed the demon's chaotic power and used it to mend the entropy of the world with sympathetic magic. It was a significant task, for if the illusions wavered or tore, the demons could break free, wreak hell upon the domains their power oversaw. Catastrophic destruction, firestorms, plagues, genocide, floods—all were possible, as history had shown.

Her fellow jailor, Zinan, scowled as she entered. He had not changed either, of course, his countenance ever youthful. The gleaming blue of his eyes belied both a penchant for mischief and an intensity that both fascinated and provoked her. Centuries past they had greeted each other with fleeting touches, harried smiles, but always pleasure. There was no welcome in him now.

"What's the matter?" she asked.

"Hephaestus keeps putting dents in his walls. He's within a few cracks of breaking out. Why hasn't he been tuned?"

Tuning was always Zinan's answer—condition the demon rather than adjust the setting.

"He doesn't need tuning." Reika gazed at the panel that illuminated the smith's prison, letting herself submerge into his reality.

FIRE AND METAL, the thunder of the forge. Boredom, curiosity.

With a touch to her crown, Reika sculpted the viscous matter of illusion.

As he battered the walls of his rocky home in Lemnos, the god of smiths came across a vein of gold—vibrant yellow, as brilliant as the locks of Aphrodite's hair.

Reika grinned. Trust Hephaestus to be distracted by the glitter of gold. She listened to his thoughts, a shadowy voyeur.

'Twill make a fine coronet for his beloved Goddess of Love. And it would not be a mere bauble, but magical. A spell to make the wearer invisible.

Hephaestus leaned on his great bellows, absorbed

in his newest project.

FAR AWAY, IN a world not contained in even a fraction of the god's imaginings, an active volcano rumbled and burped sulfurous clouds that brought early twilight to an island village. The people in the village watched, their boats ready for launch, hoping it would fret no further. They smiled in shared relief as the angry mountain subsided, contenting itself with a last grumble before returning to rest.

REIKA DISENGAGED FROM Hephaestus."See? That's all it took."

Zinan glowered. "'What an incompetent keeper you are,' says the pretty lady in dulcet tones." He adjusted the fit of his crown and turned his back to her.

"Not incompetent, although I wouldn't disagree with petulant as a spoiled child." Her answer was quiet, but in the Chamber, her words hung in the air.

"Reika, what is it?" Zinan's tone was exasperated.

"What do you mean?" She knew, but preferred feigning ignorance.

"I remember when you shouted at me with more tenderness than a dozen of these chilly exchanges hold. Why must every time we come together be so—?" Zinan reached for her, and Reika flinched away.

A flash from the World Simulacrum saved her from having to answer.

In the center of the Chamber of Command, an orb of smoky gray, terrestrial green, and glowing azure spun. It was large enough to hold a full-grown man, were it hollow, but the World Simulacrum wasn't a prison; it was a mirror. An ancient construct, created by the council of wizards and keepers after the recovery from the last cataclysm, its purpose was simple, to display the world to those who chose to seclude themselves in a windowless citadel forever: guardians, caretakers, jailors.

Now it flared in warning, pulsing once, then again.

"It's the Southern Hemisphere," Reika said, tracing her fingers over the throbbing lines of red. "The continental plates are straining. Earthquake imminent. A big one."

Zinan followed the fault lines over craggy mountain ranges and under canyons. "The focal point is going to be Botan."

"A small township. Can the population be evacuated?"

He glanced at her with a mixture of frustration and rebuke. "Perhaps it was small generations ago. It is now upwards of fifty thousand souls."

Trust Zinan to know. He had an affinity for the people, for the lives of the world, as keepers must. Reika preferred the slow, potent evolution of the inanimate—stone, air, water. It was easy to forget how quickly time affected the living.

"Well? How long do they have?" Zinan asked.

Reika sunk her fingers into the Simulacrum, let herself immerse in the construct. She loved this feeling, her body becoming the world, her heartbeat the ebb and flow of the living planet. She coasted the air currents—cold, mercury gales like a solemn chorus, rivaling a draft of alluring warmth. Here there was no Zinan, no friction or discord, just the warm stream, circling the world in a gust of thermal burn. She could spread herself to the wind and disappear for a year, or a hundred years.

Zinan's voice brought her back. "Don't float away."

"I wasn't." It was a lie. But the seduction of the moment fragmented. She shifted to ride the leaden tide that would bring her to earth, out of the atmosphere and into the heavy rock. Sinking past flourishing greenery and through bulky roots, she delved deep into bedrock smashed together by time.

She touched the apex of pressure and tension, her mental fingers exploring it, surveying it. In moments she understood the mammoth forces at work, beyond words or logical analysis. With the ease of centuries of practice, she gave the seething energies form and structure within the boundless faculties of illusion.

A PAIR OF GIANTS vied, shoulder to shoulder, for dominance. Their battle was ponderous, and their wills adamant.

SHE PULLED OUT of the Simulacrum with a familiar reluctance. "The pressure is just shy of critical."

"Why didn't the last wizard adjust this? Weren't there foreshocks?"

"No warning. The plates were locked together. He probably overlooked it, or thought it wouldn't need intervention for a while yet."

"I'll rouse the Banshee, get her to awaken Botan's populace so they'll be ready for flight." Zinan turned his attention to the far wall where a streak of blackness shuddered against a curve of panel.

Reika looked away. She didn't like the Banshee. She was erratic, capricious, flitting from malicious activity to cruel torment from second to second in her illusory prison. Zinan indulged her sadism, revealing a penchant for it that had always disturbed Reika.

Reika riffled through the demons at her disposal before deciding upon Jian Lao. He was a solid personality, being not just a manifestation of earth, but of permanence as well. It would be a simple thing to goad him to action.

Reika watched with Jian Lao's eyes, listened to his thoughts as she layered a new illusion upon his reality.

THE CELESTIAL PALACE trembled, rocking as though it would uproot itself from its foundation.

Off balance and discomfited, Jian Lao watched a monstrous fin rise from a rocky chasm and sink back like a whale breaching the ocean.

It appeared the sea monster Shachihoko had turned himself into a tiger-headed fish and now swam through the Wu Yo, the five sacred mountains, unsettling the foundation of the holy palace. That could not be tolerated.

Jian Lao summoned dragons to his side and rode upon the greatest—an imperial beast with five claws on each foot—to do battle. Confronting Shachihoko, Jian Lao wrestled him, pinning his thrashing tail while the dragons gnawed at his sides.

REIKA LEFT JIAN Lao to check on the Simulacrum. She plunged her fingers into the tectonic fault lines, groping for the lines of power that would link her to the world's core. Instead of earthy plates and bedrock, she watched the illusion she had planted.

THE GIANTS GREW tired, lulled by a force

more intent, more purposeful then they. Like a pair of squabbling children, they sulked and muttered, but were forced to settle.

REIKA RELAXED. THE compressional build-up subsided, the danger passing even as she stood there, her thoughts aligned with the sprawling world mirror.

But glancing back to check on Jian Lao's progress, she was shocked to see he was no longer triumphing against Shachihoko. He had pulled out of the combat.

Reika pitched her consciousness into Jian Lao's realm, momentarily dizzied by the frantic realignment.

THE GOD OF EARTH faltered, confounded. One of his *long*, his dragon allies, had metamorphosed into a multi-headed monster. It was foreign to anything Jian Lao has ever encountered. He stood amazed, while beside him, Shachihoko revived.

ONE OF THE cubicles bordering Jian Lao's had cracked, a tiny breach of reality bleeding to its neighbor. It wasn't enough to free either demon, but was more than sufficient for illusory borders to waver and merge. Reika identified the anomaly. The monster was a hydra—a Grecian construct in an Eastern setting—as bizarre as a sea serpent in a desert. As soon as she recognized it, she knew where to look for the outflow: Hephaestus' cube. Weakened by his earlier restlessness, hairline fractures splintered through the fabric of Lemnos.

"Zinan, there's a leak! It's causing a variance and distracting my demon. He's losing against the quake!"

Zinan spun away from the Banshee's panel. "I'll

fix the breach; you get Jian Lao on track."

Reika dived back into Jian Lao's realm, sharing her thoughts with his, and willing the god to heed her suggestions.

THE NEW MONSTER is a trick of Shachihoko, she said-thought. *Though it may look like a creature of madness, it is but a dragon in a cunning mask. See, there are the scintillating scales and the four-clawed toes.*

Jian Lao, emboldened, flipped a hand at the hydra in refutation and turned his back. He refused to acknowledge it, for he would not be made a fool of.

When Jian Lao looked away, Reika took the opportunity to lop off the hydras heads, all save one.

Jian Lao sniffed. As he thought, it was just a *long*, looking perhaps abashed at being made into Shachihoko's pawn.

But Shachihoko had had time to rest. He was strong again. His tail flailed with wicked speed, and his jaws dripped acid.

God and monster hurtled together. Shachihoko bit, his tiger teeth deadly sharp. He fastened upon Jian Lao's shoulder, ripping away flesh.

Reika stumbled, feeling the tearing pain of it. Tremors of movement beneath her feet. An earthquake in the Simulacrum. In Botan, a cluster of houses shuddered. Masonry cracked and fell. It was just a foreshock, but it heralded terrible destruction.

Jian Lao was no longer enough to quell the tremors.

Reika left the earth god and thrust into Hephaestus' panel. She shoved past Zinan busily patching cracks in Mount Lemnos.

—THE FINISHING TOUCHES on Aphrodite's coronet. It was delicate filigree, painstaking work for such massive hands. But Hephaestus was a dexterous master craftsman.

It was dangerous, but Reika had no choice. Concentrating to keep the irregularity as slight as she could, she twisted the lines of illusion.

The earth cracked apart, a glowing fissure in the ground. A lizard emerged.

Hephaestus saw six legs and smelled a rancid odor, like death on the wind. It was warning enough. He turned his head and grabbed a shield polished to a glossy sheen. He pointed it at the basilisk, which died of fright when it glimpsed its own reflection.

Before Hephaestus could wonder at this strange invasion, another scaled body emerged from the cleft. And another. He donned a helm to shield his eyes from their baleful looks, but as fast as he killed them, more appeared.

I must seal the split with stone, Reika prompted. *Before I am buried in the stinking carcasses of a deluge of basilisks.*

By touch alone, the smith worked the bellows as he aimed the shield at the murderous lizards. When the fire scorched even him, he tipped it, sending a stream of molten ore into the crack. As the basilisks writhed in the searing river, salamanders now, the smith put his shoulder against the mountain wall.

Sweat poured from his brow. His teeth ground with effort. The mountain moved.

While she concentrated, caught up in the smith's effort. A burning basilisk glared at her, glowing orange from the fire. She stiffened feeling her limbs growing sluggish from the potency of the malevolent lizard's gaze.

But of course, *it was only an illusion.*

"What is an *illusion*?" Hephaestus grunted.

SHE PULLED OUT immediately. Zinan flew with her.

"Are you hurt?" he asked, his blue eyes wide with concern. "You almost succumbed to the basilisk. Do you want me to—?"

Reika wilted before the Simulacrum. "No. I'm fine." Arms trembling, she reached up and touched the fault line.

THE GIANTS SLUMBERED. Their snores sent up mild shudders of distemper, but they were at rest.

Jian Lao bound Shachihoko in loops of granite, lecturing it all the while.

Hephaestus—

"REIKA!"

She fell back to herself, jostled from her mental dance by Zinan's voice.

Hephaestus stood in the Chamber of Command, freed from his prison. His was a familiar visage: one of his legs twisted and his face marred by scars. He had the appearance of a wax figurine held over a fire and then remolded by an inexpert artist. Undeniably ugly, but despite being crippled, immensely powerful. Muscles bulged across his shoulders and arms, a smith's physique.

Although she'd interacted with him frequently, intimately even, it had been in safety, with him contained and reacting to the stimuli she provided. Here he dwarfed the Chamber of Command with his presence. She could smell him, the burn of molten metal and the sear of sulfur scorching her throat. Heat radiated from him, surging out in rippling swells to match her fear.

"Where am I?" His voice was a shredded rasp, coming from a fire-parched throat.

Zinan, always first to synchronize with emotions and distress, stepped forward. "This is a dream, a fantasy. You are asleep."

The smith frowned. "Is this another ruse of Ares to put me aside while he dallies with fair Aphrodite? There was a scourge of basilisks to oppose me, but I have vanquished them. I go to ascend Olympus to give a golden bauble to my beloved." He looked at his empty hands. "Where is it?"

Reika glared at Zinan. Hephaestus was hers. A fantasy of dreaming would be harder to instill in a mind like his, full of action and flames and jealousy. She had no choice now but to continue with Zinan's narrative.

"You stopped in a field of poppies to pluck a bouquet for peerless Aphrodite," she said. "Red blossoms like unto the petals of her lips. But lo, the sweet pollen made you sluggish. You lay down, and now you dream a wondrous strange vision. It is, though, naught but a dream. All you need do is waken, and you can continue to beautiful Aphrodite's bower."

For a moment, it seemed it would work. Hephaestus nodded, accustomed to the cadence of her illusions, but then his eyes lit upon the crown on Zinan's head. "Thief! Thou hast stolen the coronet I forged!"

He moved faster than a lame man ought to, snatching the crown off.

"No!" Reika cried, lunging to stop him. Too late. Zinan disappeared.

Hephaestus turned the crown in his hand. "I was mistaken. This is not what I crafted." He dangled it from a finger, like a sulking boy with a broken toy.

Reika grabbed the crown back, feeling anguish tight in her chest, a keening grief that would batter her to her knees if she let it.

The crown was light in her hands, lighter than such a powerful talisman ought to be. With a wavering arm she pointed to the panel where Hephaestus' world flickered, drawing his attention. It took on greater dimension and color as she focused on it.

A BEAUTIFUL WOMAN, the Goddess of Love herself, stood among silver clouds and marble columns, white as the rising sun. Her shining hair swirled around her shoulders in a riot of curls. She smiled in greeting, offering her hand in welcome. The god of war, Ares, took it. His red sword of strife was sheathed, and his eyes gleamed. The fingers of his other hand tangled in the silk of her tresses.

"THE JACKAL MEANS to seduce her," the smith growled. "Oh, would I were there. He would not dare touch her. I would fling him from the lofty heights of Olympus!"

It was the opening Reika needed to return him to his prison.

HEPHAESTUS SCALED THE heights of Olympus, snarling at Ares. He pulled his mighty fist back.

Aphrodite pouted winsomely, rushing to cling to her husband's arm. "He was but brushing a noisome insect from my hair," she said. "But what is this? Is this lovely trinket a gift for me?"

Ares slunk away as the smith offered the golden coronet up.

REIKA WITHDREW FROM Hephaestus' reality and drooped to the floor. She would have to tune him, pare down the curiosity, the doubt that had allowed him to break out. Later.

Her eyes burned, a prickle of tears behind them.

Zinan was gone, destroyed when he was disconnected from the crown. She faced a hundred years alone. How could she keep the world spinning by herself? Reika clutched the crown to her breast. Its sharp ridges were a poor substitute for warm arms, a lover's embrace.

"Reika!"

The voice was thin, panicked but familiar. She gaped, looking wildly around for Zinan's familiar image. "Where are you?"

"I'm lost."

She could feel him, faintly, through the crown in her arms. Somehow, in the moment of severance, he had saved himself, escaped into the only reality left to him. He was in one of the demon prisons.

"There must have been a surge of chaos when Hephaestus snatched off your crown. It flung you into an illusion. Look around. Tell me where you are and I'll get you out."

"It's dark. There's a glow coming from everywhere, but I can't make out any details." She heard the fear in his voice. Once, she had been all the sanctuary he needed. "There's a cold wind."

Several panels down, a shuddering darkness bled shapes and shadow. The last illusion Zinan had molded.

"Is there any sound?" she asked. "Do you hear wailing?"

"No. Wait, yes. It's faint."

"You're in the Banshee's realm. I'll come and get you."

"How will you find me?"

A good question. "Can you make out anything at all?"

"There's a big darkness in the distance. It feels like it ought to be solid. I think it might be the mausoleum."

"The Undertaker's Citadel. Stand by the gates. I'm coming."

"Reika?"

"What?"

"How is this possible? How can I be in a demon's illusion?"

"Don't think about it. Worry about getting to the gates. If I don't get you out of there, the Banshee might kill you."

"Y—yes. I'll wait for you at the gates."

The Banshee frightened her. Reika had to remind herself not to impose elements into the Banshee's illusory reality which would confound her.

A GLOWING ROAD pointed the way to the Undertaker's Citadel. In the distance, a wolf howled, alone and desolate. A scared traveler made her way to the gates of Hell.

Stupid to have to layer all these unearthly trappings together. But if she didn't, she would surely draw the

Banshee's attention. As long as Reika posed as a background feature, she might be ignored.

The traveler walked the glowing road cowled in a black hood. It hid her face. She did not raise her head when night wings swept by overhead, for she knew better.

Before her stood the Undertaker's Gates, soaring out of the bleak mausoleum.

Reika peered into the gloom. There were the gates, but where was Zinan? At her touch, they cracked apart, groaning on rusted hinges. She passed into the Undertaker's grounds, sensitive to any twinges which would warn her of the Banshee's interest.

Zinan had imagined the mausoleum as a mansion of black marble and onyx. A single corridor led to the throne room (a parallel to the Chamber of Command?), where the Undertaker sat on a throne of bone. At his side, his Queen, the Banshee, glared out from the tangles of her hair.

Reika hovered on the verge of pulling out, but then she saw Zinan. He sat cross-legged on the raised dais, twirling something that shined dully in his hands. The Banshee hissed at Reika as she approached, but made no other protest.

Reika bent down. "Zinan, quick, take my hand."

He glanced up, making no move to reach for her. Reika saw he toyed with a crown.

"It's a funny thing, being locked in a realm of death," he said. "It makes one wonder about afterlives and the nature of flesh."

Reika pushed back hysteria. "This place is affecting you. I can feel the desolation weighing on me. Take my hand and I'll lead you out."

He continued as though she hadn't spoken. "When the council harnessed the demons, they thought they would only serve if they believed the illusions were real."

Reika eyed the Banshee. "You shouldn't say such things here—"

"Did you know she realizes we've imprisoned her in a cell of dreams? She likes it. She doesn't mind being used because she gets what she wants. It doesn't matter to her whether it's real or not, as long as it feels real."

"S–she knows?"

"Has for centuries."

"And she hasn't tried to break out?"

"Apparently not. It occurs to me, if the Banshee knows, other demons might too."

"Zinan—"

"So an awareness of the situation does not preclude service."

"Please—"

"Reika, there's no way I could have been shunted into a demon realm when Hephaestus stole my crown unless I'm—" he paused, waiting for her.

There was no point in dissembling. He had discovered the truth, as a part of her had known he would. "Unless you're a demon," she finished.

"For how long? Or have I always been one, and everything else was the lie?"

She hesitated before sitting beside him and taking his hand. It was the first time she had touched him since the accident. His fingers were solid and strong, exactly as she remembered them to be.

"Zinan, during our last cycle, Surya, the sun god, got it into his head to go nova. He couldn't be distracted by adventures and wives. You went in to tune him. You stopped the nova, but there was still damage: fires, droughts, and finally a huge solar flare. You were deep in Surya's consciousness when it happened, so close the heat spilled out. Your body burnt to ashes."

"I died?"

Reika nodded. "There was a little of you left in Surya's realm. Just a bit of magic and awareness, enough so your presence registered as demonic."

"And you used an illusion to trap it. Me."

"If I hadn't, what was left of you would have faded away. I can't spin the world by myself. But, I–I hadn't realized how difficult it would be to keep the pretense up. I couldn't even tell you why—"

"Was that all? You lied to me, kept me as your pet demon, out of your duty as Wizard of Eternal Watch?"

"No, it wasn't like that! I couldn't let you die."

His voice was empty. "Why not?"

"I–I need you. Not just as Keeper of Forever, but because I'm lost without you. I love you."

He was silent for a long while. Around them, the Banshee's reality seemed to melt away, as though it realized its insignificance in this dialogue.

"It's been a long time since we've been solace and helpmate to each other," Zinan said at last. He regarded the gold circlet in his hand. "If I put this crown on my head, what will happen?"

"I don't know. What do you want to happen?"

"I want us to be the way we were before I died. I want the world to continue turning with you and me, keeper and wizard helming her. I want to love you again. Do you think maybe—?"

"Maybe."

Zinan raised the crown and set it on his head.

THEY STOOD TOGETHER, their bodies entwined in the center of the Chamber of Command. Reika felt the warmth of Zinan pressed against her. Even though she knew he wasn't real, having the truth out allowed her to pretend. And after all, wasn't it enough to believe in a dream of happiness?

As one they reached for the Simulacrum and submerged in the world currents. Their bodies moved together, sharing a union both primal and profound as they rode the world. But before Reika could abandon herself to the shared ecstasy, a stray thought intruded. *Would she still be there if she took off her crown?*

"The Wizard of Eternal Watch" was reprinted in Best New Romantic Fantasy 2, *edited by Paula Guran (Juno Books, 2007). This story started out with a slightly longer title as "The Wizard of Eternal Watch and the Keeper of Forever"; however, somewhere along the way to its first publication, it lost its second half. There's a bit of irony there. Maybe I should write a sequel titled "The Keeper of Forever." Nah.*

MORTAL CLAY, STONE HEART

"*AI-YAH*, SHU-MEI!"

I started, nearly dropping the unfinished earthenware bowl. Baba has said—sometimes exasperated, sometimes amused—that the element that governs my spirit is not metal or fire, wood or water, but clay. And I suppose it's true. As far back as I can remember, I've had an affinity for finding the hidden grace inside pliant earth, the hard strength and flowing forms that the industry of my hands and the fire of the kiln can set free. But this affinity frequently makes me unmindful of such things as the passage of time and Baba's homecoming.

"Clay on your face, and is that slurry on your sleeve?" My father continued to scold me as I fumbled the bowl aside. "Do you think you could manage not to disgrace me with a grimy-faced welcome for the visitor I'm expecting tomorrow? The daughter of the Emperor's Overseer of Terracotta Sentinels should be refined and decorous."

"Hmpf. Do the terracotta soldiers concern

themselves with the impression they make upon me?"

"Shu-mei, you're no longer a child. Have you considered how other girls your age are already married, even mothers?"

I pretended to scrutinize the bowl, hoping that Baba wouldn't notice the heat suffusing my cheeks. I couldn't tell him my heart already belonged to another. Although I didn't delude myself that the man I admired regarded me with the slightest measure of consideration I held for him, it was too embarrassing and absurd to admit my one-sided love to anyone.

"What do I need a husband for?" I mumbled. "Kong Fuzi says that contentment can be found 'with coarse rice to eat, water to drink, and—"'

"Be silent!"

I couldn't have been more astonished if Baba had spouted hooves and bleated like a goat. "The mouth is the gateway to misfortune" was how other fathers instructed their daughters. But Baba had dismissed my nurse when I was four when she'd scolded me for demanding to be taught the abacus. He'd taught me himself how to do sums and read, and the arts of philosophy and debate.

Baba relented. "Forgive me. You couldn't have known. The Emperor has prohibited any discourse regarding the Hundred Schools of Thought."

"What?" Relief that my father was not, after all, transforming into a goat vied with shock.

"The only principles one may extol are those prescribed by the School of Law."

"That's ridiculous. How can any man prohibit another from thoughtful contemplation?"

"Qin Shi Huangdi is not a man. He is the Emperor. And he has decreed that all the histories and analects in opposition to the School of Law be consigned to fire."

The treasury of bamboo slip scrolls in my studio hung before my mind's eye. "But how can the empire move forward if it cannot study the past?"

Baba fixed me with a hard stare. "Shu-mei, I am in the habit of indulging your stubbornness, but you must understand the position I am in as one of the Emperor's officials. There can be no hint of sedition from this house."

I'd never seen my father look so grim. "I understand."

IN THE MORNING, Old Baishi, Baba's retainer, loaded our library into the firebox of the little dragon kiln built into the natural hillside at garden's edge. Bleak and disconsolate, I turned to clay for commiseration, and it obliged me with a yellow Qilin. Adorned with the antlers of a deer, the hooves of an ox, and the tail of a lion, Qilin are the celestial emblem designating the element of earth, the natural foil to water—absorbing it. And water was the element and symbol of Qin Shi Huangdi.

As seditious acts went, it was admittedly a feeble one. But it helped, venting my outrage in this manner until late into the night.

I woke the next day to the afternoon sun chiding my eyes, with barely enough time to make myself presentable for Baba's guest. I donned a malachite coat and an ebony skirt that swirled like the sea, all the while wishing for a comfortable *shenyi* and the company of clay. As I finished securing the jade-green sash, I heard the *hi-hiin* whinny of a horse.

I hurried out, rehearsing appropriate phrases of

welcome. But at the entrance, all words deserted me. It was not Baba with some stuffy official but the crown prince of the empire, Prince Fusu, handing the reins of his mount to Baishi.

Although I stood mute and stock-still, he noticed me and bowed. "No one could mistake you for anything but a refined and well-born lady today, Shu-mei."

I was goggling like a fish, but I couldn't look away. Memories of our previous meeting transfixed me, juxtaposing with this moment: Prince Fusu before me now and Prince Fusu from that other afternoon, drenched and seeking refuge from a sudden downpour.

HE'D THOUGHT ME a servant—my hair in rags, my *shenyi* splattered by clay. His first words to me, by way of introduction, were, "You, girl, could you fetch your mistress and bring me a towel? I'm near to drowning on your doorstep."

I bowed to conceal my embarrassment and irritation. "I'm Shu-mei. My father, the Imperial Overseer of Terracotta Sentinels, does not keep household servants. I'm afraid there's only myself—that is, unless you'd prefer our gardener, old Baishi, to attend you?"

"That won't be necessary," he replied, curt and dismissive. He stepped past me, and I shut the door to the rain, wondering whether I'd invited the more turbulent storm inside.

I fetched one of Baba's housecoats to replace his sopping garments and put a pot of water on to heat, aware of his eyes following me.

"You're not at all as I imagined," he said at last. "I

thought the girl who fashioned that exquisite terracotta rabbit in your father's studio and who puts his apprentices to shame with her unflagging diligence would be as stout and formidable as he. But instead I find a willowy girl with rosy cheeks."

My cheeks, however rosy they'd been, blazed.

An eyebrow quirked. "Modest too? Unpretentious, modest, and undoubtedly steadfast. If you're a fraction as diligent as your father claims, you epitomize Kong Fuzi's ideal of virtue."

"You're a follower of Kong Fuzi's teachings?" I all but lunged at the opening, anything to shift the conversation from my rosy cheeks, the merits of my character, or even the terracotta rabbit. I'd fashioned that piece after my mother died—she'd been born in the year of the rabbit—and it was not a subject I cared to discuss with this man.

"Any school that proclaims real knowledge to be in grasping the extent of one's ignorance can be assured of my devotion." Prince Fusu winked, startling a smile from me. His return smile transformed him, making him younger, warmer. Our eyes met, and something within me shifted, realigned. Shaken and off balance, I understood later it had been nothing more or less than the foundation of my world giving way to be replaced by a new one: Prince Fusu.

"SHU-MEI?" THE prince's voice shook away my paralysis.

I bowed, mortified I'd kept him waiting like a peddler at the door. "Please be welcome. My father isn't home yet, but I expect him soon."

"Until he arrives, could I impose upon you for a tour of your kiln? The rain precluded my curiosity last time."

"Of course." I joined him on the stone walkway, striving to appear composed despite the agitated tremors that shook through me. But at the garden gate, I frowned. "Oh, wait, what if Baba's stuffy official finally arrives?" I clapped both hands over my mouth, appalled. How had I let myself say that aloud?

The prince chuckled. "I wondered if I'd misremembered the girl who glared at me so fiercely when I mistook her for a servant. But at last, here she is. As to the matter of the stuffy official, I suspect I am he."

I smiled shyly back, relieved. "Your highness could never be stuffy."

"And why not? I've had the finest teachers to instruct me on all the varied forms and methods of stuffiness. I assure you, I'm a master at it."

I bit back a giggle and opened the gate.

"I've been unforgivably remiss in not thanking you for your gift before now," Fusu said, "but I hoped to be able to convey my appreciation in person."

I lowered my eyes. I'd fashioned the marbled tiger from two different clays to create a pattern that was both impetuous and considered—like the man strolling beside me.

"I showed my father your tiger," he continued, "and he wishes you to sculpt a matched team of terracotta horses for his afterlife city." The prince drew a sandstone token stamped with the imperial sigil from a pouch and offered it to me. "How convenient of my father to provide an official reason to call upon you."

I only partly heard him, my attention riveted on the imperial token. "The Emperor wants *me* to sculpt his horses?"

"He desires that his spirit world be as lively as this earthly one."

I glanced up at the tautness in the prince's voice, reminded of the whispered speculations that had arisen when Qin Shi Huangdi had first conceived his afterlife city, revealing his disquieting obsession with the trappings of immortality. Fusu would never undermine the Emperor, but his tone told me how troubled he was by his father's recent directives. The prince believed as I did in Kong Fuzi's teachings, as Baba had taught me: *Ignorance is the night of the mind.* How much more had it sickened him, the mandated destruction of wisdom?

I accepted the token. "My efforts will no doubt be inadequate, but I will do my best."

"I await with great anticipation your forthcoming masterpieces, *sifu.*"

No one had addressed me as a master artisan before. Did modesty require me to protest such honor or would that cause the prince to lose face? Before I could make up my mind, he swiveled, head raised.

"What's that?"

I strained, listening.

Rumbling, a subtle crescendo in the distance. An approaching thunderstorm perhaps?

"Men marching," Fusu said. "A brigade's worth, but not soldiers."

"Not soldiers?"

"The tread of an army is a tide that swells in a measured, beating gait." Fusu's eyes no longer saw me, focused upon some inner reflection. "This is undisciplined and irregular."

"A parade then?" I suggested.

"Shall we go see?" He pivoted and strode to where Baishi had tethered his horse, leaving me to scramble after. He flipped the reins free and mounted while I struggled not to trip over my skirt. He leaned to me, hand outstretched.

Should I have hesitated, refined and decorous like a court lady? I didn't. I gripped his hand, and he swung me up behind him.

My riding acquaintance was limited to infrequent occasions atop draft horses and once, an indulgent cow. I teetered, feeling as graceful and secure as a sack of rice on a bamboo fence.

"Don't be afraid. Hold onto me if you're unsteady."

"I'm not afraid." I hoped I sounded bolder than I felt. "But I admit to a certain unsteadiness."

"Fei-hua is as courteous as she is swift. Neither of us will let you fall."

I remained dubious, but contrary to my expectations, when Fei-hua sprang forward, I didn't topple off, a feat I credited to luck, as it certainly could not have been skill. I did, however, clutch at Fusu like a drowning woman, kicking Fei-hua with my heels in the process. Fortunately, her disposition was as gracious as the prince had said, and she didn't take offense.

I eased my grip, and, as though he'd been waiting for this, Fusu leaned forward, bringing us low across Fei-hua's back. She, in turn, transformed from an earthbound creature to one of wind, anchored to this world only by the prince's will. To call both Fei-hua and the drays I'd sat before "horses" was like calling a blue-glazed platter the sky. And what I'd taken as a gallop had actually been for her an easy canter.

I laughed in fierce exhilaration, intoxicated by the heady combination of Fei-hua's speed, the heat of Fusu against me, and the thrill of basking in both. The prince turned his head, beaming like a boy.

All too soon, we slowed. I brushed streamers of hair from my eyes and saw why. A procession of hundreds of men marched on the imperial highway; scholars all, their vocation apparent from their somber robes.

Prince Fusu slipped from Fei-hua's back and handed me the reins. "Wait here."

I didn't know if he'd addressed me or Fei-hua, but fortunately the mare considered it one and the same. I had no notion what to do with the straps of leather he'd given me, and doubted I could've dissuaded her if she'd had other designs.

Where had the prince gone? I scanned the highway until I spotted him engaged in discussion, not with a scholar, but with a soldier. Before I had time to speculate about their conversation, Fusu came pelting back.

"I regret that our visit must be curtailed," he said, hurling himself into the saddle. He waited only for me to grasp his waist before spurring Fei-hua into a breath-stealing run.

"What's going on?" I had to yell to be heard above the strident wind.

"The Emperor has ordered the execution of those scholars for adhering to Kong Fuzi's teachings."

I almost tumbled off in horror. The only thing that saved me was Fei-hua, who slowed, allowing me to regain my balance.

"Shu-mei, I must return to the palace to plead with

my father to stay this massacre. Forgive me for subjecting you to such distressing circumstances, but can you bear it a little longer? We're almost back to your home."

Shamed that consideration for me had caused the prince to delay, I released his waist. Accommodating me, Fei-hua eased to a stop.

"I know this region," I said, gathering my skirt. "I'll walk from here." It was too much to wish for a graceful dismount, but I hoped I could maintain a modicum of dignity.

"I can't allow you unescorted—"

"Nonsense. This is almost my back door. If I shouted, Baishi would come charging up with his handcart." I gave up on dignity and floundered off, landing on my rump in a swell of silk.

"Shu-mei! Are you hurt?"

I picked myself up, scowling. "I'm fine. Why are you still here? Hurry and save them."

The prince regarded me for a still moment. "You are most remarkable, Shu-mei." He wheeled Fei-hua, and they were gone in a storm of hooves.

When they were out of sight, I brushed myself off and began the hike home. Distance flown atop Fei-hua translated to an exhausting plod, made worse by the hateful skirt tangling my legs. But physical discomfort was nothing to the turmoil in my head. Those scholars. Surely Prince Fusu would be able to dissuade the Emperor from slaughtering them.

When at last I straggled through our gate, Baba came charging out, the stark lines of worry on his face flooding me with guilt. Prince Fusu's visit, the glorious ride, and the Emperor's condemnation of the scholars spilled from me in a disjointed babble.

BY EVENING, EVERYONE had heard of the four-hundred scholars executed, buried alive, and Prince Fusu's exile to the northern frontier for daring to champion them.

Baba caught me when I crumpled and rocked me as I sobbed. He carried me to my room, tucking me in my coverlet as though I were a child.

When I had cried all the tears I had, I lay awake, eyes open and mind abuzz. I didn't court sleep. When my mother died, sleep had brought nightmares, dark images that laid my grief bare on nerves already keening. Solace for me resided in wakeful activity. As soon as I heard Baba's soft snores, I rose and slipped to my studio to pray for healing and strength, the cool resistance of clay my benediction at the altar of my worktable. Immersed in my litany, immersed in clay, my head cleared.

This desolate empty place that had opened in me, I recognized it. It was the same as when Mother had died. More insights came, one after another like beads on a string. This crushing grief was not because of the scholars' deaths—a great loss and tragedy to warrant tears, yes. But what had sent me to my knees was Prince Fusu's banishment.

How shallow my character that I grieved more for a single man's exile than for hundreds of deaths. Moreover, I had no claim on the prince, had never had any claim on him. Realistically, he was no further from me in the depths of Suizhou than he'd been in the palace.

I contemplated the shape beneath my hands. Although I'd given my fingers no directive, they'd fashioned an equine's long, fine nose, big, intelligent eyes, and delicately outlined nostrils. I knew this particular equine.

"Hello, Fei-hua."

I fetched the Emperor's token, tucked into my sleeve and forgotten in the afternoon's turmoil. Tracing the roughness of the imperial stamp against the slippery sandstone, I recalled a snippet of Kong Fuzi's teachings: *One should sorrow, but not sink under sorrow's oppression*, and also, *If one takes no thought about what is distant, one will find sorrow near at hand.*

Qin Shi Huangdi was an old man. One day, Prince Fusu would guide the empire back upon the path of enlightenment. And after his inauguration, I would present him with a terracotta horse in Fei-hua's image, so lifelike one might expect it to toss its head and stomp the ground. I would offer as well another of Kong Fuzi's proverbs: *He who exercises government by means of his virtue may be compared to the north polar star, which keeps its place and all the stars turn towards it.*

DAYS UNFURLED TO months, the flowers of the calendar—orchid, osmanthus, chrysanthemum—losing their petals as I cast and recast Fei-hua in clay. Evoking nuances of gracious strength and refined swiftness tasked me to my limits, but anything less than perfection was unacceptable. I'd remolded Fei-hua's head yet again when the news came of the Emperor's death.

I donned the proper mourning attire, but inside, I rejoiced. The work on Qin Shi Huangdi's afterlife city grew fevered, and Baba was called upon to attend the funerary ceremonies, a weeks-long affair.

As I checked his satchel to ensure I'd packed everything, a courier hurtled to our gate bearing another imperial writ. Baishi, shuffling with as much speed as his creaking joints could produce, delivered it to my father, and he and I hovered at Baba's elbow, brimming with curiosity.

The document was spare, but its meaning clear to anyone versed in matters of court intrigue. The Imperial Secretariat had conspired with the youngest prince to discredit Fusu in a bid for the throne. In a coup of innuendo and forged documents, they'd presented Fusu with a letter from his father proclaiming him seditious and disloyal.

There was only one recourse for a son so dishonored. The prince had swallowed poison.

Fusu was dead.

My eyes burned, but I couldn't cry. How ridiculous I was to bawl like a child when the prince had been banished yet be utterly dry-eyed at his death.

Baba wanted to postpone his departure, but I wouldn't let him. History was littered with the corpses of hapless officials caught in the turbulence of violent succession. His constancy and worth as a servant of the empire must remain above suspicion.

Alone, I drifted to my studio, my mind estranged from my body by a juncture of white numbness. When my fist slammed into Fei-hua's clay features, I felt only surprise, as though another dictated my actions, another will that pounded the clay until all signs of careful labor had been erased.

Still under the control of this unknown craftsman, my hands mounded the clay anew, fashioning an elegant brow, expressive lips, and aristocratic nose. Recognition ran through me like a burning wire: Fusu's brow, lips, and nose—an unquestionable likeness. I caught my breath and raised my palm to wipe the features away. But a tiny incongruity made me hesitate. Was that crease about the eyes something I'd done? I shook my head. Foolishness. Of course it was. I raised my hand again. This time, I couldn't mistake it. In the space of a blink, the lips had thinned, suggesting a frown.

I touched the down-turned mouth. The contact sent a tingling intimacy through my fingers of a nature I'd never known before. I snatched my hand back and squinched shut my eyes.

"Prince Fusu," I whispered, "don't you think I'm too insignificant to haunt?"

I peeked open an eye.

One eyebrow arched higher than the other. It was the same expression Fusu had worn when he'd teased me and proclaimed me modest. An ache blossomed in my chest, the first taste of wrenching grief.

"No." I jerked around, giving my back to the clay head. "Don't. If it's vengeance you want, I'll serve you. But don't be kind or gentle. Be terrible or fearsome or nothing at all. Otherwise, I'll march out and tell Baishi to throw you into some pit or bash you flat, and I'll never touch clay again."

I waited for the hurt to fade, for the merciful numbness to seep back before I dared turn around. On my worktable, the clay face had emptied of expression and personality, just as I'd demanded.

WITHOUT MY FATHER'S comings and goings to punctuate my days, I could work unchecked save only by my stamina. Under the scrutiny of vacant, clay eyes, I crafted a body to match the head, kneading and molding until I collapsed from weariness upon the straw mat in my studio.

Grueling pace notwithstanding, this work was the easiest I'd ever done. Limbs and torso manifested effortlessly, as though I didn't sculpt the clay so much as remind it. In a matter of days, quicker than I thought possible, all lay finished and drying.

I rose from my workbench to summon Baishi, and the accumulated complaints, fatigues, and distresses of my body, disregarded this while, came alive. Bent over, hands on my knees, I waited for the sickening dizziness to ebb before wobbling outside and trekking to the little dragon.

Baishi had already removed the large bricks from the kiln's entrance and stacked them nearby. I crawled inside, edging past the firebox to the stacking floor. Crouching beneath the low ceiling, I measured the space, using my forearm as gauge. I'd never fired so many large pieces at once, and if I loaded them too close, they could fuse disastrously.

I eased out of the dragon's maw and was unsurprised to find Baishi waiting for me with a soft cloth. Wiping the soot from my face, I wondered, for the thousandth time, how he seemed to know when I needed him at the kiln.

IT REQUIRED TWO days and two nights of ceaseless blastfire to mature the clay to terracotta. Baishi and I camped outside, alternating shifts to feed wood nonstop into the furnace. He tried to bully me into letting him take two shifts for my one, but I'd have none of that. So instead, he foisted huge quantities of lumpy rice and salt fish upon me until gratitude and annoyance became the same. Exasperated, I shooed him away, preferring to oversee the final hours alone. At last, weary to the core, I cast the last stick of wood in and stumbled home, too spent to change out of my smoke-drenched *shenyi* before surrendering to sleep.

Discomfort goaded me awake—nettles and grass plastered by oily soot to tender flesh. I blinked, the darkness outside my eyelids the same as within, and fumbled for a lamp. Its wan glow caught my reflection in the bronze mirror. I yelled before I could stop myself. Hair matted by clay and ashes, face and *shenyi* layered in grime, I looked like a *yaoguai* demon from the underworld. If Baba saw me like this, he'd scold me deaf. Or summon a priest to exorcise me.

I heated bathwater and soaked and scrubbed until as much skin felt scoured off as dirt. *Yaoguai* purged, I was left wide awake. So I put on a fresh *shenyi* and tramped across the garden, bearing a single lantern to augment the moonlight. The little dragon would take as much time to cool as it had to fire, but inevitably, I would spend the next days retracing my steps between kiln and house as a feeble sop to impatience.

I groped the air above the bricked up mouth. Its breath should have been balmy as summer, but there was no change to the night's chill.

Could I have slept for two full days?

I heaved bricks aside and squeezed in as soon as I'd cleared enough space to fit. On the stacking floor, I set the lantern down and groaned.

I'd set the pieces too close. They'd fused into slag. I crept over to survey the magnitude of my failure. Would it even be possible to remove the botched mess without shattering it first?

My outstretched hand contacted warmth—not cooling terracotta, but living warmth, a body of flesh. I sprang back as the man in the kiln stirred. A crash, like a hammer upon rock, and I wondered what had fallen before darkness tossed me down.

WAVES LAPPED BENEATH me, the peaceful tide. They rocked me, lifting and falling, and as a counterpoint, a drowsy rhythm drummed in my ears: *tong-tong, tong-tong.*

Realization jolted me alert. Not tide and drum, but breath and heartbeat. I shot up. Pain lanced through my skull, and I winced, hand to temple.

"Softly. You hit your head and knocked yourself insensible. I carried you to your studio."

I knew that voice, would have known it waking or asleep, even though I'd heard it only twice before. My hand fell away, the pain forgotten.

"Fusu?" I whispered.

Somber eyes met mine, not quite the color I remembered. Touched with heat, like red-baked earth. Or terracotta. But still his eyes, still Fusu.

"They said you swallowed poison."

"Ah. Yes, I did. Imagine my surprise when I woke from that and then discovered myself lacking an essential accouterment—by which I mean my body."

I followed the tilt of his head until I grasped what I'd been too dazed to notice before. The prince was naked save for a thin blanket.

I flushed and looked away. The blanket rustled, a liquid spill, as the prince closed the space between us. Strong fingers caught my chin, compelling me back.

"You restored me, gave me this mortal sheath of perception and sensation, breath and light."

His words brushed my lips, like kisses I thought, until his mouth chased his words, and I saw I'd been mistaken. Fusu tasted of wood smoke, fire, and, faintly, the salt-bitter tang of fresh water drawn from our well. He unfastened the sash of my *shenyi* and, bemused, I marveled at the adeptness of fingers I had sculpted. He parted my *shenyi*, and I marveled at the firm smoothness of skin born in the scorching blaze of a kiln. He parted my body, and all thoughts became lost in a swell of movement and heat and joy.

I SWAM FROM a languid doze to find Fusu gazing out the window in one of Baba's housecoats—the same one I'd lent him on a rainy afternoon so long ago. That he was clothed made me shy, and I tugged on my rumpled *shenyi* before padding over to join him.

Outside, night still ruled, but its authority had waned. The sky held its breath, waiting to herald in the new ruler advancing in a golden chariot upon the horizon.

"I must go soon," Fusu said.

"Yes. To avenge your death."

He cocked his head. "Do you truly think me the kind of man to hold death as reason enough to discard the virtues I cherished in life?"

I frowned.

"And can you conceive of nothing other than vengeance, no other purpose powerful enough to entice my spirit from the void?"

"What?"

He sighed. "Shu-mei, do you recall what Kong Fuzi said about vengeance?"

I shivered. "'Before you embark on a journey of revenge, dig two graves.'"

He cupped my face in his hands. "Indeed. So why would any true disciple of Kong Fuzi desire that path?"

My heart leaped, frantic wings against the cage of my chest. "But...you're leaving."

Fusu's eyes darkened. "*Sifu*, not even your wondrous craft can make the heavens forget that dead is dead."

I broke away. "You didn't come back for me. Please, say you didn't."

"Why?"

"Because—" I balled my hands into fists, trembling. "Did I do something to invite your hatred?" I stammered.

"Not hatred, you fool, lo—"

"Don't!" I hugged myself, fighting for composure. "I-I told myself I was a fool. I was nothing to you, and I would forget you eventually. But when you died, those comforting lies were ripped away, leaving me flayed and reeling. The only way I could endure it, the only way I could survive, was to let my heart be stone. But I can't be stone if you love me."

"Would that be so terrible?"

"How could it not be terrible? Thrusting someone starving and parched to a banquet and allowing one taste, one sip before snatching it all away? It's the same, offering me words of love before forsaking me to grief." I rubbed my eyes, and my fingers came back wet. My tears had spilled unnoticed, postponed but not averted. "It's too late, it seems. Stone does not weep. Better that you hated me, that you were an evil spirit. This night will haunt me my whole life, the sweetness I'll never taste again and the knowledge of what we might have been. Even if you say you hate me now, I will know you lied, and that you lied from kindness. From love."

Fusu held me with his eyes, sorrowful and stricken. "What do you want me to do? Already dawn comes to chase my wayward shade back."

"Take me with you. Anything would be better than foundering in all the tomorrows before me, bereft and alone."

He inhaled, a ragged shudder. "If you are fixed on this course, give me one last gift. Give me your heart."

Like the other time, when he'd offered me his hand to some unknown adventure, I didn't hesitate. I took the pottery knife from my worktable and, effortlessly, as though I'd practiced it a hundred times, slit open my chest. The knife unseamed me with the same couth regard that it parted clay, producing neither pain nor blood. I lifted out my heart, although the state of it embarrassed me—misshapen, drab, and rift by faults—an altogether unsuitable gift. Yet it was also appropriate that Fusu have it, inevitable. It had always belonged to him anyway.

He accepted my heart as though it were a delicate flower or rare jewel. Reverently, he smoothed away the flaws and cracks with a few deft strokes, easily finding the harmony and balance which had eluded me. That, too, was only inevitable.

"Why is this so familiar?" I asked.

"We are bound." He breathed on my heart, suffusing it with color—warm ginger, bright vermillion, tawny red—until it was no longer mortal clay, but hard terracotta. "These acts of remaking—my body, your heart—bind us and will bind us again, choices made and yet to be made rippling out like fated echoes. Our paths are destined to converge."

I wrapped my arms around his neck. "Then let's continue to our next assignation together, with clasped hands."

"And joined hearts." Fusu drew me close and set the newly fired terracotta back in my chest.

BAISHI KNOCKED SOFTLY at the studio door, concern vying with uncertainty. Usually he knew when the young mistress visited the little dragon, just as he knew when a tree in the garden needed pruning or the flowers watering. But this morning he'd found the kiln partially opened—enough for a slender girl to slip in—without any inkling of when she'd been there.

She'd unpacked it too, all by herself. Always so impatient, that one. It must have taken her several trips to lug the terracotta pieces back to the house, when he and his cart could've done it in one. Well, she was considerate, sometimes to a fault.

He knocked again. The girl had a habit of overworking herself. What if she'd fainted or had a fever, too weak to summon help?

The door swung ajar.

"Shu-mei?" he called. "Are you asleep?"

When she didn't answer, he nudged the door wide enough to poke his head around.

Baishi furrowed his brow. "Huh. Not here?" About to withdraw, he paused, his attention caught by the pair of terracotta figures at the window. He crept into the studio, curiosity winning out.

The couple stood entwined, highlighted in a nimbus of sunlight. They were so close they might have been sculpted as a single piece, although he knew that wasn't possible. Leaning for a better look,

Baishi marveled at the exquisite detailing, admiring the girl's evident skill and masterful technique.

The maiden's face, upturned to her lover, was ethereal and lovely, radiant with joy. The man embraced her in an attitude of tender adoration, though there was a sadness about him, so lifelike, so poignant that tears pricked Baishi's eyes.

He clucked his tongue at an old man's foolish sentimentality and turned to go. On his way out, he spied the pottery knife lying on the floor. Absently, he picked it up and set it on the worktable.

The young mistress could be so heedless sometimes. She might as well be clay.

"Mortal Clay, Stone Heart" was published in the anthology The Dragon and the Stars, *edited by Derwin Mak and Eric Choi (DAW Books, 2010), which received the 2011 Prix Aurora Award for Best English Related Work. It was inspired by the British Museum's traveling "The First Emperor: China's Terracotta Army" exhibit, which I was lucky enough to see when it came through Atlanta. One day, I hope to visit the first emperor's burial mound in Xi'an.*

ABOUT THE AUTHOR

Eugie Foster calls home a mildly haunted, fey-infested house in metro Atlanta that she shares with her husband, Matthew. After receiving her master's degree in Psychology, she retired from academia to pen flights of fancy. She also edits legislation for the Georgia General Assembly, which from time to time she suspects is another venture into flights of fancy.

Eugie received the 2009 Nebula Award for Best Novelette for "Sinner, Baker, Fabulist, Priest; Red Mask, Black Mask, Gentleman, Beast" and was named the 2009 Author of the Year by Bards and Sages. *The Dragon and the Stars* anthology, edited by Derwin Mak and Eric Choi, with her story, "Mortal Clay, Stone Heart," won the 2011 Prix Aurora Award for Best English Related Work. Her fiction has also received the 2002 Phobos Award; been a finalist for the Hugo and British Science Fiction Association awards; and been translated into eight languages. Her short story collection, *Returning My Sister's Face and Other Far Eastern Tales of Whimsy and Malice*, has been used as a textbook at the University of Wisconsin-Milwaukee and the University of California-Davis.

Visit her online at EugieFoster.com.

COPYRIGHT AND PUBLICATION HISTORY

"The Life and Times of Penguin" © 2005 by Eugie Foster. Originally published in *Andromeda Spaceways Inflight Magazine*, #18, April 2005.

"Running on Two Legs" © 2004 by Eugie Foster. Originally published in *The Third Alternative*, #40, TTA Press, Winter 2004.

"Black Swan, White Swan" © 2011 by Eugie Foster. Originally published in *End of an Aeon*, Marti and Bridget McKenna (eds.), Fairwood Press, 2011.

"The Bunny of Vengeance and the Bear of Death" © 2005 by Eugie Foster. Originally published in *Fantasy Magazine*, #1, Prime Books, November 2005.

"A Nose for Magic" © 2008 by Eugie Foster. Originally published in *The Pagan Anthology of Short Fiction: 13 Prize Winning Tales*, Llewellyn Publications, October 2008.

"The Center of the Universe" © 2007 by Eugie Foster. Originally published in *Helix*, #5, Summer 2007.

"The Wizard of Eternal Watch" © 2006 by Eugie Foster. Originally published in *Sages & Swords*, Daniel E. Blackston (ed.), Pitch-Black Books, 2006.

"Mortal Clay, Stone Heart" © 2010 by Eugie Foster. Originally published in *The Dragon and the Stars*, Derwin Mak and Eric Choi (eds.), DAW Books, 2010.

25531430R00105

Printed in Poland
by Amazon Fulfillment
Poland Sp. z o.o., Wrocław